~An Ignited Passion~
Sandrine Gasq-Dion

Chapter One

"What the fuck are you doing?" Wyatt whispered. The flashlight hung from his jeans loop, as he, Sebastian and Nikolai crept through the academics building.

The farther down the hall they went, the more Wyatt's hair stood on end. Sebastian's bright idea was to break into the dean's office and steal his most prized possession - a baseball. Wyatt smelled the hallway; someone had been by recently.

"Sebastian, come on."

"It's just a few more doors down," Sebastian whispered, looking over at Nik. "You got the lock-pick?"

Nikolai raised an eyebrow.

"Of course I do, but Wyatt's right. This is a very bad idea, Bastian."

"The asshole is breathing down my neck; you know I'm already struggling. My dad refuses to pay for school unless I retract my statement that I'm gay. I can't lose my scholarship because of this guy."

"Who gives a shit if you're gay?" Nikolai sighed in frustration. "You know my dads will pay for your schooling."

Wyatt looked down the hall; school was out for summer the next day. He couldn't believe he was going along with this stupid plan. At least Nikolai seemed to be on his side. They'd met a few years ago and when he realized who Nikolai was it was a laugh riot.

Nikolai Markov, son of Vince Markov and Andrei Panchenko: One was a notorious killer and the other was the head of the Russian mob. Wyatt had laughed when Nikolai asked if he had any problems with that. 'Hell no' had been his answer, thinking of his own brother-in-law, Troy, and Troy's fellow assassins who were also Wyatt's friends. Nikolai was over six feet tall and weighed in at a whopping two hundred thirty pounds. The guy was covered in muscles and had tattoos over most of his body. They'd hit it off from the get-go.

"Wyatt?" Nikolai whispered. "Anyone coming?"

"Not yet; hurry up Sebastian."

Sebastian stopped in front of the dean's door.

"Do your thing, Nik."

Nikolai pulled the lock-pick set out.

"I swear Sebastian, if I get in trouble for this …" Nikolai growled.

"Hurry up!"

Nikolai picked the lock and opened the door. Sebastian slipped inside the office, looking for the baseball. It was on the bookshelf behind the desk.

Wyatt came in, shutting and locking the door quietly behind them.

"Someone's coming," Wyatt whispered.

Sebastian grabbed the baseball in its case. "Okay, let's go."

The door handle turned suddenly and Wyatt looked for another way out. "Out the window, hurry!"

Sebastian opened the window. The floor below them had an awning and he jumped for it. "Come on!"

Nikolai heard the shouts down the hallway. Shit, the cops were here. "Go, Wyatt!"

"No, you go; if you get caught it's going to be ten times worse!" Wyatt shoved Nikolai towards the window. "Get out, hurry!"

"I'm not leaving you!" Nikolai grabbed Wyatt's hand, pulling him towards the open window.

"Dammit, Nikolai! You're a Markov, you know what's going to happen - now go!" Wyatt pushed Nikolai out the window. He turned just as the door to the dean's office opened. Four cops stood scowling at him.

"Shit."

~~

Wyatt looked at the bars of the cell and sighed.

Jail.

He was in jail for a stupid prank that he hadn't committed alone but had taken the blame for. When Sebastian had come up with the idea, Wyatt had been uncomfortable with it immediately. Then Sebastian had talked Nik into it.

Wyatt flopped down on the cot and looked around. He *had* to take the blame; Nikolai would have been put in prison. The authorities would do anything to get their hands on a Markov. They had broken into the dean's office and taken a baseball. It had been a prank and that was all. But Sebastian had panicked, fled the scene of the crime and left Wyatt to take the rap. Because Sebastian had a scholarship and a future.

Wyatt supposed he didn't have as much to lose as his boyfriend, but shit. His dad was going to come down on him like a fucking freight train for this. Wyatt sighed and looked at the time. Two in the morning. His brother would be here soon. Wyatt had been away from the reservation for four years. Going to high school in Seattle had seen to that and now he was in college at the University of

Washington. At eighteen and a half he had good grades and a chance at a real future.

Until about two hours ago.

Wyatt heard keys rustling and then one of the police officers was coming towards the cell. He stood up and grabbed the bars, singing "Nobody knows the trouble I've seen..."

"Shut up, Wyatt."

Wyatt snapped his head to the right and saw his older brother, Sawyer, walking with his husband, Troy.

"Aw, shit."

Sawyer gave his brother a menacing stare.

"Couldn't you have put him in with some huge, burly, sex-craved men, officer?"

Wyatt rolled his eyes and jiggled the bars. "Lemme out."

"No can do little brother. Judge's out for the night, won't be back until eight in the morning for your arraignment." Sawyer smiled wickedly and looked around the jail cell. "Look at that, all the comforts of home - although you have to pee with everyone watching you."

"Everyone *who*?" Wyatt motioned to the empty cell. "If you haven't noticed, it's just me in this rat trap."

"Would you like some cheese with that whine, rat?" Troy raised a brow.

Wyatt fixed his brother-in-law with a look.

"You know somehow I thought you'd be on my side, Troy." Troy was an ex-Army sniper and now an assassin working for the government. Thanks to Sam, Dakota and Sawyer, Troy had been turned into a werewolf to save his life after being mortally injured. Troy had become one of his closest friends.

"This has Sebastian written all over it," Sawyer growled at his brother. "And don't bother denying it to me, either. Why am I not surprised that you are left holding the bag when he gets some fucked up idea in his head?"

Wyatt looked around nervously and shushed his brother. "Shut up, Sawyer! I'm almost nineteen years old and I make my own decisions."

"Yeah? Even if they're stupid ones?"

They all turned as the outer door opened and another uniformed officer made his way down the wide white hallway. Sawyer smiled and loosened his grip on the bars a bit. Nicholas Stevens was a fellow werewolf and a good friend. When he and Troy had run into trouble a few years back, Nicholas had gotten caught in the crossfire but had kept his friendship with the Queets pack all the same.

"Hey, Ben, I got this," Nick smiled at the other officer and nodded towards Sawyer and Troy. Nick waited until Ben had gone back down the hall and the door clicked shut. His eyes fell on Wyatt behind bars.

"Not a bad place for you, Junior."

Wyatt gritted his teeth. "I'm glad you all find my predicament so amusing."

Sawyer smiled and looked at his friend. "What are you doing here? I thought you weren't on until morning? Already champing at the bit to start your new job?" Sawyer elbowed Nick's side.

"Are you kidding me? As soon as the blotter rolled across my desk and I saw 'Quinton' I had to see for myself which one of you it was. Not really surprised to see Wyatt here." Nick furrowed his brows. "My first day on the job as a detective and I see Wyatt's name," he sighed. "My friends are already in jail; how does that look for me?" Nick cocked an eyebrow at Wyatt.

Wyatt went to his cot and flopped down looking at the ceiling. "Oh, just go away. I'm sure I'll see you all in the morning with huge smiles on your faces in the courtroom."

"With Starbucks coffee for sure," Troy winked. "Don't rattle the cage all night, Wyatt."

"Ugh! Get out!" Wyatt rolled onto his side and faced the brick wall. He heard their footsteps receding and sighed, staring at all the graffiti on the cell wall. Some pretty good raunchy poetry was there and Wyatt tried to remember some of it for future use.

Okay, so his boyfriend was a troublemaker. But Sebastian was a good guy most of the time. Besides, Wyatt was tired of waiting for his 'supposed' mate who he'd been told didn't exist.

All werewolves had predetermined mates and Wyatt *knew* he'd smelled his mate when he was seven years old. But over the years his family

12

had tried to convince him that he had made the whole thing up. Now, at almost nineteen, he was starting to believe they were right.

But he *had* seen him - a beautiful white wolf with chocolate brown eyes. Even at seven the reaction had been immediate. Maybe not on a sexual level, but he'd had a reaction just the same. Wyatt closed his eyes and pulled the coarse wool blanket over his shoulders; he'd have to face the music in the morning. Until then he'd close his eyes and hope for mercy.

~~*~~

Wyatt was woken up by keys jingling in the cell door. Nick was smiling at him, a set of clothing in one hand.

"You're still here?" Wyatt groused. "God, you guys are like a rash on my ass, corn on my foot, a pebble in my shoe…"

"Yeah, I got it, you little shit." Nick handed Wyatt his clothes and sat on the cot next to him. "Why do you let your boyfriend get away with this shit, Wyatt? Jesus!" Nick ran his fingers through his hair. "You are so much smarter than this."

Wyatt stood up and stretched, wincing at the crick in his neck. "Save me the speech, please, I just want a shower and some hot food."

"Well then hurry up, you have to be before Judge Phillips in an hour and he is known for making a statement. This could go very badly for you, Wyatt, so think about that the next time you let your boyfriend talk you into his wild and crazy shit." Nicholas regarded Wyatt and frowned. "And for Christ's sake, take the earring out!"

"What about my nipple piercing?" Wyatt crossed his arms in mock indignation.

Nicholas threw his hands up in the air in frustration. "Jesus! I liked it better when you *only* wore eyeliner!"

*

After taking what Wyatt could only describe as the fastest shower he'd ever had - and the coldest as well - he was shown to the dining area. It consisted of a chair with a card table. He ate runny eggs, some undercooked bacon and something that resembled sausage but at closer glance looked like a small piece of dog shit. Wyatt groaned and ate the cardboard toast instead.

He dressed in his suit and was shown to the courtroom; shame immediately flooded his face when he looked at his father. The disappointment was evident in John Quinton's green eyes. Nadine and Joe, friends who were more like family, sat next to John along with Wyatt's three brothers. Nadine gave him a small smile as Wyatt took his place on the bench up front. There were quite a few lawbreakers ahead of him and Wyatt couldn't believe the sentences being handed down to them. His hands started sweating at what could be coming his way, and for once he really hated Sebastian. Finally his name was called and he stood with his lawyer before the judge as he went over his offense.

"The dean has decided not to press charges since his baseball was returned. However, the DA has decided he wants to proceed with pressing charges against you for breaking and entering. Instead of jail time, I am going to give you community service at the Seattle Fire Department. You will begin this Friday at 5 a.m. and will continue until I am satisfied that you have learned a lesson, Mr. Quinton. There are things in life that are more precious to some than others. I will get weekly reports from the chief. Stay out of trouble, Mr. Quinton; I do not wish to see you in my courtroom again."

Wyatt flinched as the gavel smacked down. It seemed to reverberate through the whole courtroom. He turned to look at his family with a sad smile. This would stay with him for a very long time.

Chapter Two

Preston awoke to the sound of the alarms going off. The female voice coming out of the ceiling made him cringe.

"Engine....Ladder."

Grabbing his turnouts he flung himself out of bed and slid down the pole to the floor below. He had just enough time to grab the rest of his gear and get on the truck before they pulled out onto the busy Seattle street. Preston watched downtown Seattle flash by and sighed.

When he'd moved here from Denali, he had done it to be closer to Wyatt Quinton - his mate. Eleven long years had gone by since the day he'd shielded Wyatt from an angry and vicious Carson Drake in the woods. Since Wyatt had been so young, Preston had asked his family to discourage Wyatt from thinking he had found his mate. All that time he had waited to take what was his and when Wyatt had turned eighteen, Preston thought that day had finally come. He had gone to find Wyatt at school to tell him they were mates.

To his shock and horror, Wyatt was in the arms of one Sebastian Price who was currently the quarterback of the University of Washington Huskies football team. Sebastian was loud and proud and certainly not in the closet. Preston sighed and looked at all the buildings flying by. Wyatt would be at the firehouse for his court appointed community service today, a brilliant idea that his friend Nicholas Stevens had come up with and Preston had agreed to. They both talked to the judge and he jumped on board.

Preston knew it would allow him to spend time with his mate and try to show him there was more to life than Sebastian. That guy didn't give two shits about Wyatt and was constantly getting him into trouble, whether it was fighting at clubs or on the football field.

Wyatt had become more beautiful over the years. His black hair had been cut short for football but his eyes remained the same - those big, beautiful green eyes. Wyatt had filled out quite nicely, too. At six feet, he had a broad chest and back and was built with chiseled biceps and well-defined abs. Preston had been jacking off to that vision for years on a nightly basis.

Once he had seen Wyatt shirtless at football practice and had to stop himself from running down onto the field, growling that Wyatt was his. As it was, it took everything he had to keep his lupine side hidden at all times. Now it was becoming a mission to not only take Wyatt away from Sebastian, but for Wyatt to fall in love with him not knowing that they were mates. Preston wanted Wyatt to fall in love with him on his own, not because they were fated to be together.

"Dalton!"

Preston was snapped out of his thoughts by his chief. Chief Webber was a good guy. He knew

Preston was gay and had no problems with it. In fact, most of the guys didn't care. As long as he showed up for work and fought fires, they didn't give a shit.

"Yes sir?"

"Get your head out of the clouds, we're here."

~~*~~

The alarm went off at four in the morning and Wyatt smacked it off the night stand. He rubbed his eyes and groaned, getting out of bed. He hissed as his feet hit the cold floor. He'd packed his bag the night before so he could just get up, shower and head out. His skin prickled and then a scent wafted under the door. Wyatt opened it before Nikolai even knocked.

"Damn, you're good," Nikolai grinned.

"It's four in the morning, Nik," Wyatt yawned, stretching his arms out.

"I know, and I'm sorry. I realize you have community service today. Look man, I just want to say how sorry I am about all this. I'm heading out to Russia this morning and I didn't want to miss the chance to say goodbye. I'm trying to get Bastian to come with."

"You didn't do anything, Nik. In fact, you were willing to sacrifice yourself. We both know how the cops would have treated you if they'd gotten their hands on you. I appreciate you trying to take the blame with me."

"Look, I don't know what's going on with Bastian, but I will find out one way or another. He's been my best friend since elementary school; he befriended me when no one else would."

"Gee, I wonder why?" Wyatt laughed, sidestepping Nikolai's playful punch.

"He's not himself right now," Nikolai sighed, running a hand through his hair. "I've never seen him act so recklessly."

"From what I hear, that's your job."

"Within reason," Nikolai chuckled. "I know you need to get ready, so I won't keep you. If you need anything, you call me, okay? I want us to stay friends."

Wyatt hugged Nikolai's massive frame. Even though he was only an inch or two shorter, he was dwarfed in Nikolai's arms.

"Take care, Nik. You're a good guy and a good friend."

"Don't tell anyone." Nikolai poked Wyatt in the chest.

Wyatt put his hands in the air in mock defense. "Never."

~*~

Wyatt stood in front of the fire station and waited for someone to open the door. Five in the morning. Unbelievable. After taking a lecture from his dad for over an hour after his court appearance, all Wyatt had wanted to do was go back to his dorm room and pass out for a few weeks. No such luck. He was standing in front of a fire station at five in the morning because he'd done something stupid. Again.

Wyatt had avoided Sebastian's calls at every opportunity. He really didn't want to talk to Sebastian right now or listen to his sorry excuses for leaving him behind. The door opened and Wyatt turned to see a guy a bit older than himself. Black hair with blue eyes squinted at him, giving him the once over.

"Um, hey, I'm Wyatt Quinton? I'm supposed to start my community service here today?"

The guy nodded and yawned, opening the door. He wandered off scratching himself and mumbling under his breath, leaving Wyatt to find his own way. Wyatt walked around the quiet fire station and took it all in. He'd always wanted to be a fireman - his first toy had been a fire truck.

"Kind of quiet."

"Yeah, the guys are out on a call. I'm Austin Jacobson, better known as probie."

"Probie?" Wyatt tilted his head and raised an eyebrow.

"Yup, the new guy. I'm still on probation until I can prove myself." Austin ran a hand through his spiked hair. "So I welcome you, Wyatt Quinton. Thanks to you, they might lay off me for a while."

"That doesn't sound good." Wyatt walked around the row of lockers looking at all the helmets and boots. Equipment was spread out along all the walls of the firehouse which, true to form, were painted red. "So, are they coming back soon?"

"There's a big fire over on the pier. Some warehouse went up in flames, so it could be a while before they come back. I just came on shift myself. I'm on three and off three."

"Three hours?"

Austin laughed loud. "Oh hell no, three *days*."

"Oh." Wyatt felt his cheeks redden. "So is there anything I should start doing while I wait?"

Austin looked around. "Not sure. Chief put Dalton in charge of you." Austin shivered. "Dude, I feel for you."

"What do you mean?" Before his question could be answered, Wyatt heard the garage door opening and a very loud truck was backing up into the far side of the garage. Whoever was driving it eased the big rig in like it was a Prius. A group of men jumped out of the back and then Wyatt's heart stopped in his chest. A blond guy jumped out of the driver's seat and barked orders at some of the other guys.

Their eyes met when he turned. A look passed between them and Wyatt felt the hairs on his arms and back of his neck stand up. Jesus, but he was fucking drop dead gorgeous! Not an inch less than six foot three and rock hard muscle from head to toe. Blond and beautiful strode over with a relaxed confidence that Wyatt would kill for and he felt his hands begin to sweat. When he opened his mouth, nothing would come out. Wyatt saw the smirk on the blond guy's face. Those smoldering brown bedroom eyes were laughing at him.

"You Quinton?"

Wyatt nodded and put his hand out. "Um, yeah, I mean yes. Wyatt Quinton. I was ordered..."

"Yeah, yeah, I know. I'm Preston Dalton. I'm in charge of you for however long the judge sees fit, so drop your shit and clean the truck." With another smirk, Preston jerked his thumb towards the rig they had just gotten out of. "It needs to be washed then waxed."

"Huh?" Wyatt looked mouth agape at the monster fire truck covered with mud.

"Haven't you ever washed a car? There's a hose on the side of the building and all the stuff to wash her is in that first cabinet," Preston pointed towards the row of cabinets by the end of the truck. He took his jacket off and threw it on the bench in front of a row of lockers.

Preston watched as Wyatt just stood there, mouth open. Jesus, the shit he could do to that mouth. Hell, he thought, the things he could put in it.

"Yo! Quinton."

"Yeah, I'm on it." Wyatt made his way towards the truck mumbling under his breath.

"What's that?" Preston smiled; he could hear Wyatt calling him a jackass among other things. Werewolf hearing did have its perks.

"Nothing, boss. I'll get right on it."

Two hours later, after Wyatt had gotten most of the mud off the monster truck, the alarms went off in the firehouse. Men came down the pole and Wyatt watched in awe as they all slid down, one after another. Preston, or "Attila the Hun" as probie told Wyatt he was called, was the first one down and running right towards him.

"I'm not done!" Wyatt looked at the truck again then back at Preston.

"Don't have time," Preston pushed Wyatt out of the way and grabbed his helmet. "Move it guys!" Preston jumped in the cab and smiled down at Wyatt. "Better hope we don't run through mud again." Preston looked at Wyatt's face; Jesus he wanted him even more than before.

"You can start on dinner for the guys. Everything you need is in the kitchen."

"Wait!" Wyatt had to yell over the engines loud roar. "What do I make?"

"Figure it out, service boy," Preston winked and rolled out.

Wyatt felt his anger rising. "Service boy? Oh, *hell* no."

Wyatt gritted his teeth and looked for the kitchen. He found Austin at the long table reading a book. "I was told I had to make dinner, so what do I make?"

"I don't know, what do you know how to make?" Austin sat back and watched Wyatt rummaging through the cabinets and three refrigerators.

"I can make awesome lasagna, would that work?" Wyatt found all the pans and looked through the pantries. He found sauce, cheese, meat, noodles and various spices. "Good, everything I need is here. How many pans should I make?"

"With these guys?" Austin arched a brow. "How many pans do we have?"

Wyatt sighed. "I get it."

Four hours later the guys were back from their fire and Wyatt was pulling six pans of lasagna out of four ovens. A group of freshly showered men were filing into the kitchen, mouths watering.

Wyatt grabbed the pans and put three on one side of the table and three on the other. Within ten minutes all six pans were empty and Wyatt felt lucky to have gotten one plate. All in all, thirteen men sat around the table. What were the odds that he'd be seated with Preston right across from him? Wyatt couldn't stop looking at him. When their eyes met, Wyatt looked away from the intense stare and subsequent sneer directed at him from Preston.

Wyatt got to know most of the men in the short time they were all sitting around the table. Most of them were pretty nice and asked why he was there. Wyatt decided if he was going to be spending a lot of time with these guys, he may as well come clean.

"Dude, are you fucking crazy?"

Sean Knight, the red-haired fireman everyone called 'Big Red' laughed at him and Wyatt blushed.

"I know it was stupid. Trust me. I'm paying for it now."

"And you'll keep on paying, service boy." Preston stood up and looked at the table of men. "Let's get some rest guys, fires don't wait on anyone." Preston looked at the mess on the table and smiled at Wyatt. "K.P. duty, Quinton, clean this shit up."

"What?" Wyatt looked at Preston incredulously. "You can't be serious!"

"Hey, Preston - Chaz, Cole and I can help the guy out," Sean said.

"No." Preston looked right into Wyatt's eyes and leaned into his face. "Come see me when you're done and I'll show you where you're sleeping tonight."

Two hours later, after sweating profusely and cursing like a trucker; Wyatt had finished all the dinner dishes and cleaned up the kitchen. He set up all four coffeemakers, making sure they were filled to the brim. He was going to have to go shopping. The coffee they had was like brown mud and in Seattle you had way more options than this sludge.

Wyatt made sure all the lights were off and walked through the fire station looking for Preston. He found him in the TV room asleep in one of the chairs. Preston had a tribal tattoo on his right bicep that Wyatt didn't recognize. Even though he was Native American, he hadn't really bothered to look into his heritage - a fact his father had brought up more than once.

A smooth, tan chest lay barren for him to admire and Wyatt's eyes took in the impressive size of Preston Dalton. His blond hair was hanging slightly in his eyes; his breathing was slow and even. Wyatt put him in his early twenties at the most. He cleared his throat and Preston didn't even flinch. He tried again, a little louder this time, and was rewarded when Preston cracked open his sleep-filled eyes.

"Um, I'm done." Wyatt looked at Preston's well defined abdominal muscles and swallowed hard. A soft patch of blond hair started right below his navel and disappeared under his sweat pants.

27

Wyatt watched as Preston stood up, twisted and stretched his large frame from side to side. Wyatt started at the sight of a big black wolf on Preston's right shoulder blade.

"Nice ink."

Preston turned and looked at Wyatt. "Let's get you to your bed, service boy. Another long day awaits you." Preston threw his shirt over his right shoulder, hiding the black wolf with green eyes. He made his way up the stairs and pointed to a door.

"That's the shower and right down the hall is your room. It's not much but at least you don't have to sleep with a bunch of guys who snore."

"Can I ask you a question?"

Preston turned to look at Wyatt and felt his body responding. He closed his eyes and took a deep breath; God he wanted to grab Wyatt and devour him.

"What?"

"What's your deal? I know I fucked up and I'm here to fix that, so why do you feel the need to make it even harder on me?" Wyatt looked into Preston's eyes and felt his skin break out in a fine sheen of sweat. Jesus, but the man was beautiful, everything about him called to Wyatt.

Ignoring his head, Preston's dick led him closer to Wyatt and he leaned over him, looking deep into his eyes.

"You don't think before you act, Quinton. You could have a record for what you did.

Breaking and entering is a serious crime. You took something that didn't belong to you and even though you gave it back you caused a man a great deal of pain. Did you know that Dean Smith's father was at that game with him? His dad caught the ball for his son and it's the one thing he treasures, a last gift from his dying father. Think about that tonight."

Preston made his way down the hall to his room and turned to take one last look at Wyatt.

"You are going to have to think about what's more important: A guy who will drag you into doing something you know is wrong or standing up for yourself for what's right. I may seem like an asshole, but life isn't easy."

Wyatt leaned up against the wall and sighed as Preston's door shut.

"God, I'm an asshole." Wyatt dragged his tired body into the room and shut the door. A twin bed sat against the wall and a small bookshelf held several titles Wyatt had never read. There was a small dresser on the other side and the walls were bare. He looked around and found his bag had been put in the corner. Too tired to take a shower, he fell on the bed and closed his eyes. Tomorrow would be a better day. It had to be.

Chapter Three

The next day and the three weeks after that had been a nightmare. Wyatt was cleaning toilets with a toothbrush, mopping floors, washing and waxing the trucks, making dinner for all the guys and then cleaning up after them. He hadn't had a chance to call anyone or do anything else but work, work and work. His body was protesting just getting out of bed in the mornings. He had no idea how these guys got up at all hours of the night and day, running to put out fires. He kept a safe distance from Preston, not that it mattered much; any time he saw Preston his heart rate increased and sweat covered his palms.

Wyatt did his chores and kept his contact with Preston to a minimum, hanging out with Sean or Austin instead. The beginning of the fourth week, Wyatt had just finished waxing the truck he called 'hell bitch.' She shone like the sun and Wyatt smiled and made his way into the kitchen. He flopped down on a chair and looked at Preston reading the newspaper. He had strong hands. Wyatt could almost feel them running down his body. Ugh, he didn't want to think of Preston like that. His body, however, wanted Preston twenty four hours a day; it was a bit unsettling. Wyatt had never had sex. He was stubbornly waiting for his mate.

"I'm all done."

Preston looked over the paper and smiled wickedly. "You sure about that?"

"Yes, I'm sure. I just put the last coat of wax on her." Wyatt stood up and made his way back down to the garage and stopped. His heart fell into his stomach and the anger rose inside him so fast he felt his teeth elongating. "Son of a bitch," he whispered. The truck he had just spent four hours washing and waxing was covered in mud again. Wyatt felt Preston's presence behind him and he turned on him as soon as his teeth receded.

Preston smiled; Wyatt's eyes had changed. "You missed a spot."

Wyatt's hands curled into fists and he turned on his heel and went for the door before he shifted. "Fuck you, asshole!" Wyatt slammed the door open and walked into the street promptly running into a wall. A wall named Sebastian.

"Wyatt!" Sebastian picked him up and kissed him hard.

Wyatt pushed Sebastian away and wiped his mouth off. "Get off of me! Because of you I'm stuck in fucking hell, Bastian! How could you do that to me? Leave me there to take the fall for your stupid fucking idea?"

Sebastian took Wyatt around the side of the firehouse and pushed him into the wall. He ran his hand through Wyatt's hair and kissed his lips. "I'm sorry, baby, but you know I can't get caught doing anything like that. I'd lose my scholarship."

"What about me, huh? I had something to lose, too!" Wyatt pushed Sebastian away from him. His anger deflating, Wyatt sighed. "This isn't working for me anymore, Sebastian."

Sebastian leaned into Wyatt and ran his hand over the front of his jeans, squeezing. "Your mouth says one thing but your dick doth protest a bit much." Sebastian turned Wyatt around and pushed his face into the wall, brushing his cock against Wyatt's ass. "Come on, baby, you didn't even let me fuck you."

"Get off of me, Sebastian." Wyatt felt the building's bricks slice into his cheek. "You're hurting me."

"Yeah? I'm going to hurt you so much more, Wyatt; you don't get to end things with me. Not after months of waiting for you to put out." Sebastian pushed his cock harder into Wyatt and bit his ear lobe. "Come on, right here. Let me fuck you."

"Get the fuck off of him. Now." Preston stood nearby with his arms crossed.

Sebastian eyed the man looking at him. "Who the fuck are you? This isn't any of your goddamn business."

"I'm the guy who's going to put you down so hard you'll be crying for your mommy. Now get the fuck out of here before I pick you up and throw you out." Preston advanced slowly looking at Wyatt. "You okay, Wyatt?"

Sebastian pushed Wyatt harder into the wall. "I'll call you later, Wyatt. We can talk without interruption."

Wyatt watched Sebastian cross the street before he went back into the firehouse. He could feel Preston walking right behind him and his lupine side was fighting to come out. He was pissed, and hurt. How stupid had he been? Years he'd been friends with Sebastian, and they'd only started dating recently. Sebastian had just been waiting him out to fuck him. He felt like a fucking idiot. "Just go away, I have to wash the truck."

"I'll get the probie to do it; slow down Wyatt." Preston ran to catch up.

"Just leave me alone, Dalton. I don't need your fucking commentary right now, okay?" Wyatt tried to get into his little room but Preston's foot slid between the door and the jamb. "Jesus, you've done enough today!"

"Just let me look at you, okay? He shoved you into the wall pretty hard." Preston could see the cut was already healing and a wild, panicked look hit Wyatt's eyes when he realized the same thing.

"It's okay, Wyatt, I know what you are," Preston said softly.

Wyatt stopped breathing and looked into Preston's eyes. "W-what do you mean?"

Preston pushed his way into the tiny room and closed the door. "I said I know what you are;

I'm friends with Nicholas Stevens. I know you're a werewolf, Wyatt; I won't tell anyone."

"H-how do you know that? " Wyatt sat on the bed and looked up at Preston. "How long have you known about us? I mean werewolves?"

Preston smiled and leaned against the wall, crossing his legs at his ankles. "A long time, I'm okay with it and all. Nick's cool, we hang out and stuff so..." Preston shrugged his shoulders.

"Is he like your friend or something else?" Wyatt could feel his cheeks heating; as much as he hated to admit it, he was attracted to Preston - in a real bad way.

"Are you asking me if I'm gay, Wyatt?" Preston had to smile. Wyatt's eyes were finding something interesting on the floor and his cheeks were a bright red.

"Um, well... I...just, you know..." Wyatt could feel the room getting smaller, if that was possible.

Preston moved closer and Wyatt stood up and backed into the wall. Preston felt his heart racing as he closed the distance between them. He stood right in front of Wyatt and pulled his face up with his fingertips. "Yes, I'm gay and no, Nick isn't my boyfriend. There is only one man for me, Wyatt. I'm just waiting for him to grow up." Preston ran his thumb softly over Wyatt's cheek and leaned in, looking into those beautiful green eyes. "Goodnight, Wyatt." Preston walked to the door, turning at the last second. "Oh, and Wyatt?"

"Yes?"

"Lose the earring."

"Can I keep the nipple piercing?" Wyatt smiled mischievously as Preston seemed to shiver.

"Not a good idea in the house, Wyatt. Goodnight."

Wyatt watched Preston as he left and collapsed on his bed staring at the ceiling. His body was going through all kinds of emotions. He was upset and hurt that Sebastian had used him all this time, and excited and horny from Preston being so close to him. Preston had said there was only one man for him so why did he get so close? Was he that man? Wyatt was more confused than ever; they had just met. How could he be the man for Preston? Wyatt sighed and closed his eyes, he'd think about it tomorrow.

~~*~~

Preston awoke to sunlight filtering into his room. He had slept through the night for once. No alarms had gone off, no medical emergencies. His body was sore and needed a good run through the woods. Being around Wyatt made it even more difficult to hide his lupine side. His pack alpha, Wayne, had taught him how to mask his scent from Wyatt and right about now he was grateful for it. Wyatt wanted him. Preston knew that as sure as the damn day was long. But it wasn't enough just yet. Wyatt had to fall in love with him. It was all or nothing as far as Preston was concerned.

35

He looked at the time and saw it was quarter to nine. He was going to have to shower and get his ass in gear if he was going to meet Nick at Wenatchee National forest. He looked in on Wyatt on his way to the shower and saw he was still asleep. He was even more beautiful when he slept. Preston sat on the edge of the bed and ran his fingers through Wyatt's soft hair. Wyatt's lips were perfect for kissing and Preston couldn't help but run his fingertip softly over Wyatt's bottom lip. Wyatt whimpered and Preston backed away quickly; he made his way back out into the hallway and ran smack into Big Red.

"Hey, what's up?" Preston smiled at Sean. The guy was huge and he had to look up at him even though he himself was six foot three.

"You were kinda hard on the kid, weren't you? How do you expect him to fall in love with you when you treat him like that?" Sean smiled. He'd been close to Preston since they came on together as probies. He knew all about Wyatt Quinton. He also knew about Preston. That happened by accident. They had been in a fire and a large chunk of ceiling had fallen, landing right on top of him. Preston had pulled it off of him like it had been a board. Right then he had known something was different about Preston Dalton and when Preston confessed, Sean had laughed - until two seconds later when he was staring at a white wolf. Not so funny after that.

Preston leaned against the wall and looked at his friend. "I have to do what I have to do; there's a thin line between love and hate. Wyatt needs to know that Sebastian's an asshole, although I think he caught of glimpse of that already," Preston sighed and ran his hand through his hair. "At least I know he didn't sleep with the guy."

"No shit?" Sean looked shocked. "Well that's a plus right? He's still pure for you, just like you are for him." Sean waggled his eyebrows.

"Oh shut up, you don't have to remind me that I've saved myself for Wyatt. Every time we go out to the clubs it's easy for me to stay faithful to him - slim pickings out there," Preston smiled and punched Sean in the arm. "And even if there *was* someone who caught my eye he'd never be Wyatt."

"Aww, that's so fuckin' sweet, Dalton." Sean side-stepped Preston's next punch and grabbed his arm. "Come on, food's going to be gone if we don't get our asses to the kitchen."

"Food? But Wyatt's asleep."

"He was up at five this morning making breakfast for the crew; everything's in the oven on warm." Sean smiled when Preston looked at Wyatt's door. "He made lunch and dinner, too."

Preston felt his heart aching. God he wanted to hold Wyatt, kiss Wyatt. It would have to wait. "Okay, let's hit it."

After breakfast Preston showered and made the drive to the park in his Jeep. He pulled into the parking space next to Nick's big Ford diesel truck and jumped out, smiling at him. "Hey you, how's it going?" Nick had been the one who helped Preston find his apartment when he first got to town.

Preston had pined for Wyatt for years, and after his friend Riley Flynn-Esposito had gotten the whole, soapy story out of him, Riley had loaned him his jet periodically so Preston could go see – well, watch - Wyatt in Seattle. And after that, well, Preston couldn't bear to stay away.

Now being in close contact with Wyatt, trying to mask his scent so Wyatt wouldn't know he was his mate was draining him. He needed a good run, and badly.

Nick smiled and made his way over to Preston's Jeep. "It's good. I talked to the judge yesterday and he told me to tell you it's up to you when he releases Wyatt. Although I don't think Wyatt has plans for the summer; he spent his last day of school in jail," Nick chuckled.

"Yeah, well his birthday is coming up," Preston looked around at all the trees, the smell of pine was strong and his body was buzzing with anticipation. "I want to do something special for him but I want to make sure Sebastian's out of the picture. He might be. The asshole actually told Wyatt he had only been with him this long for sex. How fucked up is that? As horny as I am that's not

what I want from Wyatt; I just want *him*. Period."
He had to admit he had wanted to take Sebastian
and beat him within an inch of his life for even
putting one finger on Wyatt. Just the thought of
Sebastian kissing Wyatt had Preston's skin
crawling.

"Well let's take a nice long run and clear our
heads. I'm pretty convinced I'm never going to
find my mate at this point," Nick sighed and took
his shirt off, looking out at the forest. He was
starting to give up on the notion of a mate.

"Well, hopefully he won't be seven years
old when you do," Preston cracked up and clapped
Nick on the shoulder. "Let's go."

~~*~~

Wyatt woke up to the blaring sound of the
alarm and the sound of boots on the floor. He got
up out of bed and threw his sweats on with a fire
station shirt, courtesy of the chief. He made his
way to the kitchen and looked at the mess on the
table and counters. With a loud sigh he cleared the
table and put all the dishes in the industrial size
dishwasher. He found a note from Preston on the
fridge giving him his chores for the day. At least
one of the chores wasn't washing the hell bitch.
Wyatt sat at the kitchen table and looked around
the room. School was out and now he had no idea
what he was going to do for the summer. He

thought about going home but after his incarceration he didn't have the heart to face his dad. Wyatt smiled when Sean came into the kitchen with bags of groceries.

"Hey, Big Red," Wyatt stood up and grabbed one of the bags. "Please tell me there's coffee in one of these bags."

"Seattle's best," Sean smiled pulling a bag of ground coffee out. "How are you doing this fine morning? Thanks for the grub by the way. Preston ate two plates before he left to meet Nick."

"Preston's with Nick?" Wyatt couldn't help the jealousy creeping into his voice. When did he suddenly care what Preston Dalton did? *You have for a while, dumbass.*

"Yup, went up to the park just like they always do. I think they fish, or bird watch," Sean shrugged his shoulders. "I don't know, never went with them." Sean smiled at the look on Wyatt's face; jealousy did not suit him. "I'm usually the one he takes to the bar with him, although I can safely say my type isn't there."

"Huh?" Wyatt snapped out of his thoughts. "What do you mean?"

"Preston's gay, I'm not. We try to go to one of his clubs one night then one of mine the next. It's kind of funny to get hit on, though," Sean chuckled and leaned against the counter. "You can see the guys salivating when they find out I'm a firefighter; it's good for my ego."

Wyatt looked at Sean and could see why he got hit on. He had to be over six foot four, had short red hair and the bluest eyes Wyatt had ever seen. Sean's biceps were the size of Wyatt's thighs and he had an ass you could bounce a quarter off of. Wyatt's thoughts strayed to Preston's body in comparison - there wasn't any competition there. Preston had a body that made Wyatt's prick hard just by looking at him. He didn't get that with Sean.

"So, does Preston get hit on, too?"

"Are you kidding me? The minute we walk in all eyes are on him. It's that blond haired, sexy brown bedroom eyes look he's got. He's got to beat them off with a stick." Which was the truth and Sean could see Wyatt getting angry. "He's picky, though."

Wyatt looked up at Sean. "Picky?"

"Oh yeah, he likes them young and Native American," Sean winked and walked to the kitchen door. "I've got some stuff I gotta do. Just yell if you need me for anything."

Wyatt stood at the counter with his jaw hanging open. "Young and Native American?" Okay, he didn't need a building to fall on his head, but come on. Preston had been an ass to him. Except for last night, which still had Wyatt confused. Wyatt shook his head clear and made sure the kitchen was spotless before heading off to do the rest of his chores. An hour later he sat on the couch in the TV room half asleep when Austin walked in with a big grin.

"What?"

"Hey, a bunch of us are going out to the club tonight, ya wanna come?"

"Which one? I can't get in you know." Wyatt sat up and rubbed his hands over his face.

"Gay bar up on the hill and you don't need an ID when Sean's with us, he knows all the bouncers. Just can't drink, so you in?"

Wyatt thought about it, he'd finished everything on the list - which hadn't been as much today, thank God. Dinner was already in the fridge and just needed to be warmed. Wyatt stretched and stood up, smiling at Austin. "Sure, why not."

A loud crash could be heard in the garage and Austin and Wyatt looked at each other. They took off running and found a guy looking around the fire station while righting an oxygen tank that had been knocked over.

"Hey, who are you?" Austin tilted his head.

"Kurt." Kurt extended his hand to Austin while eyeing Wyatt. "It's my first day. Can you tell me where the chief is?"

"Just Kurt?" Wyatt looked the guy over. Short brown hair with a slight wave at the edges, sapphire blue eyes and the guy obviously worked out.

Kurt narrowed his eyes. "Are you checking me out? Look, I don't do dudes, okay? That shit freaks me out."

Wyatt gave Kurt a sneer. "You're not my type."

"It's Kurt Maguire, and I'm everyone's type."

Wyatt snorted and waved his hand in the air. "Whatever."

The chief came out and put his hand out to Kurt; Wyatt narrowed his eyes as they left together. He felt Austin's eyes on him and shot him a glance.

"What?" Wyatt put his hands on his hips.

"You don't like him."

"He's a homophobic jerk."

Austin laughed loud and clapped Wyatt on the back. "Oh God, wait until tonight!"

Wyatt rubbed his hands together with a gleeful grin. "Yes, that will do just fine."

Chapter Four

Preston leaned back against the bar of Cuffs & Stuff Club watching the dance floor. Chaz had been watching a cute little blond for quite a while now and Preston laughed; the guy was shaking his ass, making it very obvious that he wanted Chaz to dance with him. The club was packed as always, bodies everywhere pressed tightly together. Preston had been to his share of gay clubs in Alaska, which wasn't too many. Seattle on the other hand was brimming with gay clubs. The lights pulsed and Preston's eyes wandered to the front door. Sean was talking to one of the bouncers and Preston saw Wyatt right behind him with Austin and another guy who didn't look familiar.

"Shit, Sean brought Wyatt," Preston looked over at Chaz.

"Well here's your chance to hold him in your arms," Chaz smiled and stood up looking around. "I think I'll take the blond up on his offer."

"Wait!" Preston grabbed Chaz's shirt. "How did you—"

"Please," Chaz rolled his eyes. "It's so obvious, Dalton."

"Keep your clothes on," Preston waggled his eyebrows.

Chaz laughed and winked. "Rawr."

Preston looked back towards the door and saw Sean making his way over with a huge smile on his face. Preston sighed and watched the dance floor again and that's when he saw Sebastian. He was in the back corner with a dark haired man and they weren't talking.

"Son of a bitch," Preston muttered. Preston looked around to find Wyatt. He was standing across the room talking to Austin all while shooting looks his way. Preston smiled at Wyatt and he actually looked shocked. Preston had to laugh at that; he crooked his finger at Wyatt. Just watching Wyatt move across the floor had Preston's cock hard as a rock; he tried to relax and make his boner go away.

"Hi," Preston smiled as Wyatt stopped in front of him.

"Hi," Wyatt looked Preston over. Hot damn the man looked good. Faded blue jeans hugged him in all the right places as did his skin-tight black T-shirt. "So, um, you want to dance?"

"To this?" Preston smiled as the music got louder and changed beat.

"Unless you can't shake your ass," Wyatt shrugged and walked backwards onto the dance floor, shaking his ass.

"Oh hell," Preston pushed away from the bar and made his way out onto the dance floor shaking his hips towards Wyatt. He made his way closer and put his hands on Wyatt's hips, digging his fingers into them. Wyatt's eyes widened and Preston pulled him into his chest. "Now, we can dance."

"Um, this isn't dancing," Wyatt felt Preston's lower body brushing against his cock and fought for control. "This is more like grinding."

Preston smiled and released Wyatt only to get behind him and grab his hips again. He leaned over and brushed his lips over Wyatt's ear. "Yeah? Does it bother you? It's just dancing, Wyatt."

"More like fucking on the dance floor," Wyatt mumbled. The music was blaring and he closed his eyes moving his hips to the beat, feeling Preston's hands tight on his hips. He was more than a little turned on. Preston's hands moved lower on his hips and Wyatt leaned back into Preston's hard body letting his head fall back. Their bodies moved together to the beat and Wyatt felt Preston's cheek on his own. His pulse was through the roof and he felt a warm hand sliding up his shirt, searing the skin on his side. Goose bumps popped out all over his body as Preston's hand slid up slowly.

Preston nuzzled Wyatt's cheek. Wyatt's eyes were closed as they moved to the music and Preston turned them to face the opposite side of the club. Sure enough Sebastian was still in his make-out session in the corner. "When I tell you to, I want you to open your eyes, Wyatt. Then I want you to see with your heart what I see with my eyes. You are worth so much more than you know." Preston took a deep breath. "Open them."

Wyatt opened his eyes and let them adjust before he took a look around. Couples were dancing all around them and then he saw Sebastian in the corner, with a guy, kissing him like no one was around. In that moment he didn't know whether to be upset or relieved. Then the anger kicked in. He had spent almost a year with Sebastian, putting up with his shit, listening to him whine. Wyatt felt his teeth itching in his gums and then Preston's grip tightened on him. "That's what you wanted me to see?"

"He doesn't deserve you, Wyatt, he never did. He used you, got you into trouble and then moved on to his next conquest. You deserve someone who loves you, cherishes you - don't you see that?"

Wyatt shook Preston loose and turned to face him. "You don't know anything about me!"

"That's where you're wrong, Wyatt, I know everything about you. So what are you going to do now? Ignore what's right in front of your face?" Preston saw Wyatt's skin ripple and pulled him into his chest, he lowered his mouth to Wyatt's ear. "Keep it under control, Wyatt; pull it back. I think these people would scream if a two hundred pound wolf was suddenly in the club."

"I do *not* weigh two hundred pounds," Wyatt had to chuckle. "I top out at one eighty. Anyway, I'm going to go over there and tell him what I think - so you can stop lecturing me now." Wyatt looked up at Preston and smiled. "I'll keep it in check." Wyatt pulled away from Preston and felt the warmth leaving his body, warmth he hadn't realized he craved - and that warmth was coming from Preston Dalton, a man who knew what he was and didn't care.

Wyatt made his way over to Sebastian in the corner and tapped him on the shoulder. "I don't think we've met." Wyatt put his hand out to Sebastian's make-out partner. "I'm Wyatt Quinton, Sebastian's ex-boyfriend, and you are?"

"Wyatt, what are you doing here?" Sebastian led Wyatt away from his date. "I didn't expect to see you out at the clubs."

"Obviously or you wouldn't be swapping spit with some other guy," Wyatt smiled and clapped Sebastian on the back. "I'm happy for you. You've moved on. Now, if you'll excuse me."

"Whoa, no way." Sebastian grabbed Wyatt's hand. "You don't walk away from me until we talk about this. This was just me blowing off steam, I needed a warm body and that was all."

Wyatt laughed loud. "Yeah, well your warm body is moving on to the next warm body. Better get back to him." Wyatt yanked his hand out of Sebastian's and made his way to the bathroom. As soon as he opened the door, he was shoved into the bathroom and pushed up against the wall. Sebastian's breath was on his ear and the smell of alcohol and anger flooded the small space of the bathroom. "Get off of me, Sebastian."

"I told you, you don't get to say when we are over, Wyatt. You made me mad, I retaliated with another guy and that's all it was."

"I never knew you were so abusive, Sebastian." Wyatt felt Sebastian's arm across the back of his neck, he wasn't worried about Sebastian hurting him. He was six feet tall and weighed one hundred eighty pounds. Granted Sebastian was taller and weighed more but Wyatt had been trained by his brothers-in law, he could wipe the floor with Sebastian. Plus, the whole wolf thing gave him super strength. "Get off me, this is becoming boring. I said it's over, Sebastian. Take your ass home."

"I don't think you heard me," Sebastian growled in Wyatt's ear.

"Oh, I think he heard you just fine," Preston slammed the bathroom door shut. "Take your fucking hands off of him right now."

"Walk away asshole, this doesn't concern you." Sebastian eased his arm off Wyatt's neck. "This is the second time you've put your nose where it doesn't belong."

"I'm giving you five seconds before I haul you out by your hair and make you look like an idiot. Now let go of him before I really get angry." Preston walked towards Sebastian slowly, his hands out at his sides, fingers moving with anticipation.

"Wyatt's my boyfriend; I'll do what I want." Sebastian smiled and pushed away from Wyatt.

Preston tilted his head and smiled. "That's where you'd be wrong, Sebastian. Wyatt is mine and he's always been mine. Now unless you want to see just how violent I can get, I'd suggest you leave right now."

Sebastian assessed the man in front of him, his hands were out and ready and the look in his eyes was almost feral. He didn't like his odds. "Fine."

Preston stood still as Sebastian walked by him to the door. He kept his back to the door as Sebastian opened it and stepped back out into the club. Preston lowered his hands and looked at Wyatt. "Are you okay?"

"I don't need saving you know, I can take care of myself and I think we both know I could snap his neck like a twig." Wyatt leaned against the bathroom wall and took a deep breath.

"It's not a matter of strength I'm worried about. Sebastian is abusive on so many levels," Preston sighed and ran his hand up Wyatt's bicep. He could feel the muscles rippling under his touch. "Come on, let's get back out there."

"What did you mean when you said I was always yours?" Wyatt turned and looked at the shock on Preston's face. "Yeah, I heard that part. I was standing right here."

"I was just, uh, trying to get him to back off." Preston cursed under his breath. His lupine side had taken over for a split second. "Come on," Preston put his hand out to Wyatt.

Wyatt smiled and put his hand in Preston's. The sudden jarring of a memory had him gasping. He was seven again, the forest was spread out all around and little wolf Wyatt was sitting, protected, underneath a large white wolf. The vision dissipated and Wyatt opened his eyes to see Preston looking at him, concerned.

"What?"

"You okay? You kind of went somewhere else." Preston took a deep breath and pulled his scent back, the altercation with Sebastian had caused him to slip.

"No, I'm good." Wyatt tried to get a feel for Preston but couldn't smell anything on him but arousal. Interesting. Very interesting.

They made their way back over to the crowded bar and Wyatt cocked an eyebrow at Kurt. The guy was looking at him like he was some kind of disease. "Problem?"

"Nope," Kurt looked out over the dance floor.

Sean leaned over and looked at Kurt. "I don't know where you transferred from, but we don't tolerate homophobia in this firehouse, dude. We are all brothers and we watch each other's backs. If you can't be part of the team, we can't trust you."

"I'm fine, okay?" Kurt rolled his eyes. "I'm just not used to guys touching each other and shit."

"Where the fuck are you from?" Preston cracked up.

"Wyoming." Kurt looked at the group of men.

"Ahhh," all of them nodded and said together.

The rest of the night was spent with Austin, Sean, Kurt and Chaz. They danced until the club closed then went back to the firehouse. Wyatt took a shower and closed his eyes as the water washed the club and Sebastian off of him. It was over with Sebastian and Wyatt had to admit that even though he had been pissed off at first, he felt nothing but relief now. His thoughts went to Preston instead.

Preston Dalton: blond-haired, brown-eyed bombshell. His skin still felt Preston's touch on him, like it was seared into his skin. Wyatt's prick was hard and he closed his eyes, stroking himself and thinking about Preston's hands, the touch of his lips. It didn't take long before Wyatt was shooting all over the bathroom wall.

He leaned his head against the cool tiles and let a long, deep breath out. He hadn't cum that hard in a long time; he and Sebastian had played around but it had never gotten past the kissing stage. He had never wanted Sebastian to give him head and Wyatt wasn't going to go that route with a guy who wasn't his mate. Some things were best saved for the man he was supposed to be with for life. The halls were quiet when Wyatt finally left the bathroom. He had almost made it to his room when Preston came around the corner and stopped in his tracks. Wyatt realized he was standing in the middle of the hallway in a towel.

"Um, goodnight, Preston," Wyatt opened the door to his room and paused before going in. "Thanks for what you said tonight."

"I meant it, Wyatt, you deserve so much more." Preston made his way past Wyatt to his own room.

"What about you? What do you deserve?" Wyatt looked at Preston's back. He had stopped walking and now was turning slowly to face him.

"I deserve someone who loves me and only me. Someone I can love with my whole heart above anything or anyone else. It's the same thing you deserve, Wyatt, someone who brings you up and not down and who takes your needs into account above his own. That's love, Wyatt, not what you and Sebastian had."

"I never loved him." Wyatt walked to Preston and stood in front of him. "There's something about you, though," Wyatt whispered. "I don't know what it is but something's there."

Preston looked down into Wyatt's eyes and saw his hand moving to Wyatt's cheek; his thumb caressed Wyatt's bottom lip. "My God, you are so beautiful, Wyatt," he whispered.

"No one's ever called me beautiful before." Wyatt looked in Preston's eyes. So many emotions flickered behind those brown eyes: need, want, fear. "Why are you afraid?"

Preston backed away, once again he was letting his emotions out and he couldn't do that. That led to his lupine side getting out of hand. "I'm not. Goodnight, Wyatt."

Wyatt sighed and watched Preston go to his room. God, he had wanted to kiss Preston; why didn't he kiss him? Jesus, he felt like he was twelve instead of almost nineteen. Something was there, though; he could see it in Preston's eyes. Preston felt something for him and he knew it. Wyatt went into his room and sat on the bed; his cell phone showed twelve missed calls and a shitload of missed texts. He'd deal with all of it in the morning. He was out before his head even hit the pillow.

~~*~~

Wyatt rolled over to find his phone lit up and sunshine beating on his face through the small window in his room. He grabbed his phone without looking at the caller ID and flipped it open. "Hello?"

"Jesus, you *are* alive!"

Wyatt chuckled and lay back on his pillow; his friend Olivia's voice was like a screeching car. "Ow, please stop screaming."

"Are you hung over or something?"

Wyatt could hear her giggling. He had met Olivia his first year of college in English lit, she was outgoing and loud, his perfect match in a

54

friend. They hadn't spoken much since he had started dating Sebastian. To say Olivia hated Sebastian would have been an understatement. She was a five foot four terror and made it known to Sebastian that she hated him with every snarl of conversation she had with him. Wyatt loved her to death, she had a protective streak a mile wide and he protected her from guys who wanted only one thing from her. Not that he could blame them; if he was straight he would have asked her out. She had long black hair which caressed a beautiful, cream-colored face highlighted by icy grey eyes. "To what do I owe this lovely phone call?"

"Are you still at the fire station for your community service?"

"Yeah," Wyatt sat up and ran a hand through his unruly hair. "Why? You want to go for some coffee today?"

"I'm at the front door."

"What?" Wyatt jumped off the bed and opened the door, making his way down the hall. He thought about taking the pole down to the floor below but he hadn't mastered that just yet. He took the stairs two at a time instead. "What are you doing here?"

"I wanted to see my best friend," Olivia smiled as Wyatt threw open the door. "I think we can hang up now."

"You look good, Liv," Wyatt smiled with the phone still up to his ear.

"Can I come in or do I have to stand out here all day?" Olivia snapped her phone shut and tapped her foot at Wyatt.

"Oh, yeah come on in. I think it's okay for you to be here." Wyatt looked around the mostly quiet firehouse. It seemed as if all the guys were sleeping in. "Let's go in the kitchen."

Wyatt led Olivia to the kitchen. He put breakfast in the oven and poured her a cup of coffee. They sat at the table and Wyatt played with his cup not knowing what to say; he had let Sebastian take over his life, pushing Olivia right out of it.

"Liv…"

"Don't say it, Wyatt, I'm still here and I'm still your friend. I don't care if that jackass hates me. I'm not letting him push me completely out of your life." Olivia took his hand. "I care about you."

Wyatt was just about to open his mouth when Austin sauntered into the kitchen shirtless, in sweat pants. He was rubbing the sleep out of his eyes and his mouth dropped at the sight of Olivia seated at the kitchen table.

"Um, hey Austin, coffee's on and breakfast is in the oven. This is my best friend, Olivia. Olivia, Austin." Wyatt smiled at Austin's shocked look.

"Shit, a chick in the cock house," Austin looked at Olivia and then back at Wyatt.

"Yeah, well my foot is going to be in your cock if you call me a chick again," Olivia furrowed her brows and eyed Austin.

Austin's face broke out into a smile. "Oooh, she's got teeth."

"Yeah? And I bite," Olivia winked at Austin and smiled devilishly when his face turned a bright red. "I thought firemen were tough, Wyatt?"

Wyatt smiled as more of the guys started showing up for breakfast, eyeing the petite dark-haired woman at the end of the table. One by one they all sat down and nervously picked at their breakfasts, heads down, trying not to make eye contact. Wyatt almost laughed out loud. You'd think they'd never seen a girl before. Kurt stopped at the doorway to the kitchen and tilted his head looking at Olivia.

"Well that wasn't there before," Kurt raised a brow.

"Lord, what is that smell? My dick is hard as a rock. Someone open one of those magazines with a perfume thingie in it?" Sean walked into the kitchen and stopped.

"Morning, Sean, this is Olivia. Olivia, this is Sean but everyone calls him Big Red." Wyatt watched Olivia checking Sean out.

"Um, yeah, hi, they call me Big Red cuz I'm tall and well …" Sean shuffled his feet running his hand through his hair.

"Big?" Olivia smiled and eyed Sean from head to toe. "Yes, I can see that you are." Olivia's eyes settled on Sean's hard on, tenting in his sweat pants.

"Aw, shit man," Sean turned around and faced the counter. "Um, excuse the language. So what brings you to the house, Olivia?"

"Well, Big Red," Olivia enunciated 'big.' "I came to see my best friend and make sure he threw his trash out. Mainly an asshole named Sebastian." Olivia heard gasps all around the table. "What? Did I say something?"

"Well, you said, and pardon my French," Austin stammered, "Asshole,"

"Well, shit, none of you have ever heard the fucking word or what?" Olivia cracked up when the whole table erupted in laughter. "My dad is military. I heard the word 'fuck' like five hundred times a day."

"Oh, I like her," Austin smiled and sat forward, clasping his hands together.

"Probie!" Sean's voice boomed in the kitchen. "Get yer ass down to the rig and wash it."

Austin frowned, looking at Sean. He looked back at Olivia and smiled. "Maybe I'll see you again?"

Olivia looked at Sean and saw him looking at her; his eyes darted between her and Austin. "Oh, you will see me again," Olivia smiled at Sean and winked. "I love gingerbread."

Wyatt and Kurt spit their coffee out, as did three others at the table; the loud coughing covered up the laughing at the color on Sean's face - it matched his hair.

"Holy hell, Liv," Wyatt cracked up. Whistling could be heard down the hall and Wyatt recognized the tune; it was Preston. The first lyric came out of his mouth as he came into the kitchen.

The whole table fed him the next lyric: "*Up in here, up in here!*"

Preston's eyes fell on the woman at the end of the table and he smiled. "Well now, it looks like there's a hen in the fox house." Preston smiled at Wyatt, as he grabbed his cup off the counter and filled it with coffee.

"What is with the chicken references?" Olivia sighed.

"A mare in the stallion stable?" Preston offered. "A goldilocks in the bear house?" Preston sat at the table, and put his feet up on the chair across from him. "I thought it smelled too good in here."

"No shit," Sean sighed and realized he had said it out loud. "Fuck."

Olivia giggled and looked at Preston, putting her hand out. "Olivia Stetson, and no, I don't know anything about the cowboy hats."

"Good, I hate country," Preston put his hand out. "Preston Dalton, to what do we owe this wonderful visit, Miss Olivia Stetson?"

"Well, like I said to Sean and Austin and well, the rest of the guys, I came to make sure my best friend had gotten rid of some nasty baggage. I haven't seen him for a while because said baggage made sure Wyatt never got my calls." Olivia arched a brow at Wyatt.

Preston nodded in agreement. "I have seen said baggage and I agree, the set does not match and the one piece needs to go."

Wyatt sighed and sat back in his chair. "I am not a piece of luggage, besides, Sebastian was cut loose remember?" Wyatt glanced over at Preston.

Olivia watched Preston's eyes. They were looking at Wyatt with what could only be described as love. Olivia cleared her throat. "So anyway, I thought we'd take one of our famous walks along the beach today with an ice cream. What do you say, Wyatt?"

Wyatt looked at Preston, his eyes were smoldering and Wyatt felt dizzy. "Is that okay? I mean I have dinner and stuff already done."

"Go on and have fun," Preston smiled and turned his attention back to Olivia. She seemed to really like Wyatt and it was obvious she cared about him. "It was nice meeting you, Olivia. I hope to see you again soon."

"Oh you will." Olivia shot a mischievous smile at Sean. "Bye-bye, boys."

Preston watched as Wyatt and Olivia left holding hands and laughing. He was happy Wyatt had a good friend to be there for him. He was going to follow them nonetheless, he didn't trust Sebastian and even though Wyatt was strong and could take care of himself, Preston wasn't taking any chances.

"Well, she seemed sweet." Preston had to smile at the look on Sean's face. He seemed to be in a daze. "She seemed to really like you, Sean." The whole table erupted in laughter and Sean flipped Preston the bird. "Oh come on, Red, she took a liking to you."

"Well I acted like a fool," Sean sat back and crossed his arms. "You'd think I'd never been with a woman."

"Maybe you haven't been with the right one." Preston stood up and looked at the table of men. "Well, let's get a move on before we can't."

~~*~~

Wyatt watched the water lapping at the shore and realized just how much he had missed their walks along the beach. Boats were all over the Sound today with their passengers either fishing or just lounging around taking in the warm Seattle sun. Wyatt had always loved Seattle, it wasn't that he hadn't loved living on the reservation, but it was its own world and Wyatt wanted to see what was beyond it. He smiled as Olivia licked her ice cream, she had her shoes in her other hand and was scanning the beach for shells. He really had missed Olivia. They had clicked from the first day they had met when she had said he had a fantastic ass. He in turn had said he was gay and she had then said it was a shame because he could stop traffic.

"I really did miss you, Liv. I'm sorry that I let Sebastian keep us apart but it's over now and for some reason I'm not even sad about it."

Olivia stopped and turned to face Wyatt. "I know what that reason is. Preston Dalton." Olivia saw Wyatt's face and had to smile, he was blushing all shades of red. "He's gorgeous."

"I know," Wyatt sighed and sat down in the sand. "He's so…God, I don't even know how to explain Preston, he was such an asshole to me when I first showed up at the firehouse, but then when Sebastian showed up I saw another side to him, you know? He knows me in a way I didn't think anyone would." Wyatt leaned back on his elbows and crossed his legs at his ankles. "We were dancing the other night at the club and I had all these feelings." Wyatt remembered Preston's hands on his skin, the way it felt to be in his arms. "Can you fall in love with someone in under two months? Is that even possible?"

"I think it is." Olivia smiled and licked the side of her ice cream before it dripped on her shorts. "I believe in love at first sight, though. I'm a hopeless romantic."

They sat and talked for hours about everything and Wyatt couldn't have been happier to have his friend back. It was one of the things he had been missing for months. When the sun was starting to set, Wyatt walked Olivia back to her car and kissed her cheek. He invited her to the firehouse barbeque and Olivia jumped on it. Wyatt knew that was because of Sean, he watched her drive away and made his way back down to the beach watching the sun set over the water. Pink and purple hues fell over the rippling water and Wyatt sighed at the simple beauty of the setting sun. The hair on the back of his neck stiffened and he turned to see Sebastian walking towards him. The guy just didn't get a fucking clue.

"Go home, Sebastian, I said we were done and I meant it."

"Not until I talk to you."

"Look Sebastian…" Wyatt cocked his head to the side. And then there it was; that scent he had smelled so long ago, but this time his body's reaction was much different. His cock was hard in seconds flat and his eyes went monochrome. His mate was nearby. Wyatt pivoted in the sand and that's when he saw him; the white wolf was behind him, teeth bared and fur rising on his haunches as he looked at Sebastian.

"Um, I think you better go Sebastian." Wyatt turned to see Sebastian's back as he ran. He hadn't even said anything, why would he? It just showed Wyatt he had made the right decision. Wyatt turned to see the wolf backing away from him. "No, please don't leave!" Wyatt made his way closer and felt his teeth elongating. The white wolf took a tentative step closer and Wyatt crouched down looking at him. "Please don't leave, I know it's you - the white wolf I saw when I was seven; you protected me, shielded me. You are my mate. Please don't run away."

The wolf came closer and Wyatt put his hand out waiting for the wolf to nuzzle him. He needed that contact, needed to know he wasn't seeing things, making them up and when the wolf's fur finally touched his fingers Wyatt knew. This was indeed his mate. The tears flowed as Wyatt wrapped his arms around the wolf.

"I knew it, I knew you were real." Wyatt had no concept of time as he cried into the fur of his mate. Years of wondering and finally the time had come. His mate was in his arms.

Wyatt pulled away from his mate's neck and looked into his brown eyes. Everything was there, unconditional love, want, need. Wait, brown eyes? Wyatt tried to get closer and his mate backed off.

"Wait, please don't leave. I need to see you again." Wyatt looked as his mate tilted his head then huffed quietly. Wyatt smiled and put his hand out. "Okay, I take it that means we will see each other again." Wyatt closed his eyes as his mate nuzzled his face and neck. When he opened his eyes his mate was gone, a white blur running down the beach.

Wyatt took his cell phone out and called the first person who came to mind - his brother Grayson. The phone rang twice before Grayson's husband, Taylor, answered. "Hey, Taylor, is Grayson around?"

"Yup, how you doing, Wyatt? You get soap on a rope yet?" Taylor cracked up on his end.

"Oh, ha fucking ha, Taylor." Wyatt had to smile at his brother-in-law's sense of humor, though. He was a good guy and madly in love with Grayson. Wyatt waited for his brother to get on the phone and he rolled his eyes at Grayson's laughter; obviously Taylor was attacking him in some fashion. "Sheesh."

"Hey little shit," Grayson laughed.

"Well, guess what big brother? I saw my mate tonight." Wyatt waited for some kind of reaction from his brother and heard nothing but silence. "Gray, did you hear what I said?"

"What do you mean you saw your mate? In human form?" Grayson shot a look at Taylor on the bed next to him.

"No, just like I've always said, he's a white wolf. I was on the beach tonight and he showed up just as Sebastian did. I saw him, I felt him; it's him, Gray. It was my mate."

"I'm so happy for you, Wyatt. When will you see him again?"

"I don't know but he made it clear that I would. I don't understand though, if he's my mate how come I couldn't hear him?" Wyatt chewed at his lip. "Does that mean something? Like maybe we have to have sex or sumthin'?"

Grayson cracked up and leaned into Taylor. "No, you just do. I heard Taylor loud and clear.

Maybe you just need to spend time together, you know, when he's in human form?"

"Maybe," Wyatt looked at the time. "I gotta get going back to the firehouse. I'll call you sometime this week if my boss gives me time to breathe."

"Wait, what's he like? Your boss?"

"Preston?" Wyatt smiled and closed his eyes bringing up a vision of Preston. "He's like nothing you've ever seen before. I mean he's just beautiful, you know? He's got all these muscles and his hair is like the color of clean hay and he's got these eyes…" Wyatt sighed.

"Sounds like you have a thing for your boss." Grayson winked at Taylor.

Wyatt's eyes flew open. "Oh, I gotta run bro, love you."

Grayson hung up the phone and looked at Taylor. "He's falling in love with Preston."

Taylor pulled Grayson on top of him and grabbed his ass. "Gimme some love, sugar."

"Well, alrighty then." Grayson attacked his husband's lips.

Chapter Five

Wyatt got back to the firehouse close to ten, it wasn't that far of a walk for him and he needed that time to think. He'd found his mate, or his mate had finally found him. The connection was strong and the feelings were there so why couldn't he hear his mate's thoughts? Wyatt came in through the back door of the house and tiptoed up the stairs to his room. Preston's light was on and Wyatt walked to his room and knocked softly on the door.

"Yeah."

Wyatt cracked Preston's door and peeked in. "Is it okay if I come in?" Wyatt's eyes roamed Preston's bare chest and his dick was up wanting a peek, too.

"Sure," Preston got out of bed and walked over to Wyatt. "Everything okay?" God, but Wyatt looked beautiful and when Wyatt had sunk his fingers into his fur at the beach he'd finally felt at home. "You seem, I don't know, flustered?"

"I saw my mate tonight." Wyatt looked at Preston's broad chest and swallowed hard. "Everyone told me I imagined him when I was seven, but I knew I hadn't. I saw him tonight and he came to me."

"Oh, well I'm happy for you then. Nick says some werewolves never find their mates. You must be happy you finally found yours."

"I should be and in a way I am, but I can't stop thinking about you." Wyatt inched closer to Preston. "I should be happy and yet when I came back here I wanted to see you. I think about you all the time, Preston. I wonder what it would be like to kiss you because when you put your hands on me it feels like I'm on fire from your touch." Wyatt walked closer and stood right in front of Preston. He put his hand on Preston's chest and saw the goose bumps pop up. The skin was hot and Wyatt moved his other hand to rest on Preston's pectoral muscle.

"Your skin is so hot and smooth." Wyatt leaned forward and brushed his lips across the soft skin on Preston's chest. The scent was intoxicating and Wyatt felt his dick harden in his jeans. "Everything about you makes me want to kiss you, feel your hands all over me. So why is it I find my mate, but I want you?"

Preston's hands were shaking at his sides and the urge to kiss Wyatt was getting stronger by the second. Wyatt looked up at him just then and Preston groaned, pulling Wyatt's face up to his own. Just looking at Wyatt's lips made Preston want to taste him. After waiting eleven years, he wanted to know what it was like to kiss his mate. His thumb rubbed Wyatt's deliciously full bottom lip.

"Do you want me to kiss you, Wyatt?"

"I do, I want to know what this is because I can't stop thinking about you, wanting you, needing you." Wyatt moved both hands up Preston's chest and locked his fingers around Preston's neck. "Please, kiss me."

Preston closed the remaining inches between them and brushed his lips softly over Wyatt's; his skin went up in flames. Wyatt whimpered and then Preston couldn't hold back anymore. He was vaguely aware of taking Wyatt's shirt off and they were skin to skin. He wrapped his arms around Wyatt and picked him up. Wyatt's mouth opened in a gasp and Preston slid in, taking his mate's mouth. The heat in the room was like a four alarm blaze. Everything crackled around them as the energy pinged from their bodies. Preston let out a loud moan in Wyatt's mouth. "Oh God, I want you so much."

"Preston..." Wyatt whimpered as Preston took his mouth again, the warm mouth investigating his, tongues rubbing, teasing, and sliding over one another. Wyatt felt like he'd pass out not only from the heat but from the utter pleasure he was getting just from kissing Preston. Their cocks rubbed against each other through jeans and sweat pants and Wyatt wrapped his legs around Preston's waist. "I want you."

They broke from the kiss breathing hard, foreheads pressed together. Preston took in a deep breath and tried to put his thoughts together to form a coherent sentence. Just kissing Wyatt had knocked him for a loop. He wanted Wyatt naked on his bed, tasting every inch of that tanned, soft skin.

"I want you too, Wyatt, but not here. Not in a firehouse full of men. I want us to be alone."

"Okay," Wyatt nodded his head. That was the only word he could form at that moment. Every kiss he had ever had with Sebastian paled in comparison to Preston's. His body was going haywire just being in Preston's arms. Wyatt pulled away to look into Preston's eyes and saw what looked like love there, but it couldn't be - they had just met. The brown eyes looked right through him into his soul and Wyatt felt his heart beat in his ears.

"When?"

"After the barbeque this weekend, I'll make you dinner, okay?" Preston reluctantly put Wyatt back down on the floor and caressed his face. He had to have one more taste of him. He moved his hand to the back of Wyatt's neck and threaded his fingers through the soft hair, pulling Wyatt's face up to his.

"I love your lips," Preston whispered, brushing his lips across Wyatt's and sliding his tongue across Wyatt's bottom lip. "The way you taste, I could kiss you all night and it wouldn't be enough. Tell me, Wyatt, how do I make you feel? Does your heart beat just a little faster or is it pounding in your chest when I touch you? Does it hurt when you are away from me? Like something's missing but you're not quite sure what it is?"

"Drunk, pounding, yes, oh God, kiss me again." Wyatt's eyes closed as Preston's tongue slid into his mouth again; his dick was so hard it was drilling a hole in his pants. Preston's hands were sliding up his bare back as the kiss became passionate again and then Wyatt was hanging onto Preston with both hands. His legs shook and his head spun as Preston dove deep, taking his mouth in a kiss so explosive Wyatt's whole body was dripping with sweat and his breathing was labored. Their lips moved and their tongues met and Wyatt's legs were going out by the time Preston broke the kiss. Wyatt wrapped his arms around Preston and sighed against his skin.

"I don't want to let go."

Preston kissed Wyatt's head, running his nose through the delicious scent of his hair. He took Wyatt's hand and looked into his eyes. "I promise we will be alone, okay? You should get to bed though, all right?" Preston walked Wyatt to the door. He had to get him out before he lost all control. "Goodnight, Wyatt," he whispered.

Preston watched Wyatt walk to his own room and turn to look at him. Preston smiled and Wyatt walked into his room and shut the door. Preston leaned up against his own door and took deep breaths trying to control his lupine side. It was getting harder to mask his scent and hearing Wyatt crying on the beach had almost done him in.

71

He'd wanted to shift and show Wyatt that he was his mate. Preston ran his fingertips over his tingling lips, he could still taste Wyatt, feel his heat seared into his skin. He'd always loved Wyatt, now he was in love with him.

On the morning of the barbeque, the entire crew was in the kitchen cooking. Ribs were marinating, burgers were handmade and chicken was slowly roasting. Wyatt was running around the kitchen making sure the ovens were all ready for the enormous amount of food that was going to be served. Potato salad, chili, cornbread and all sorts of other side dishes sat on the table. The grills were all up and ready in the back of the firehouse. Coolers lined up against the building were filled not only with beer but every soda you could think of. Kids were running all over the place as the chief had opened up a hydrant for them.

Wyatt leaned against the wall smiling at all the kids running through the water. He knew his time here was almost up; he had been at the firehouse for almost two months now and in that time he had fallen in love with Preston. It was crazy, you were supposed to fall in love with your mate and yet he couldn't stop thinking about Preston. His father was coming to the barbecue, along with his brothers and some of the Denali pack. Nick was making his way up the street in his patrol car, siren blasting for the kids' amusement. Wyatt waved as Nick got out of the squad car, arms full of dishes. Wyatt ran down to help.

"Hey, what is all this?" Wyatt laughed trying to juggle Tupperware.

"The whole block comes out for this." Nick shifted a paper bag to his hip. "How have you been Wyatt? The judge tells me Preston gave you a glowing report."

"He did?" Wyatt smiled and looked at the firehouse. It had become a home to him now. Preston had become home. Wyatt looked at Nick and tried to figure out how to broach the subject of mates. "Nick, do you always know when you meet your mate? I mean is it like this lightning bolt that hits you?"

"I wish I personally knew kid, but from what I hear it's like that. You get this shock in your body and it goes haywire and then you can't think about anything else but your mate," Nick stopped and looked at Wyatt. "Why, do you think you've found your mate?"

Wyatt looked at the firehouse. Preston was out front with a couple of the guys, he was shirtless and in shorts shaking his ass to the music blaring from the boom box. "Yeah, I think I did."

More and more people showed up as the morning turned into afternoon; it seemed as if all of Seattle was at the firehouse. Wyatt watched Preston's movements throughout the morning. The thought of being alone with him tonight had his skin buzzing with excitement. He wanted to kiss him, feel Preston's hands on his bare flesh. Music blasted, all the guys lined up to dance to "Party Up" by DMX and Wyatt almost pissed his pants as they did a dance for the crowd. Preston rolled his hips in a slow circle and Wyatt's mouth dropped open as Preston's hand traveled down his chest slowly. There were twenty other men standing with Preston and Wyatt didn't see any of them; his eyes were focused on the man he was in love with. He was so focused on Preston he didn't see his family show up until he heard Sawyer's voice in his ear.

"Well, hot damn, baby brother. No wonder you want to stay here for more service," Sawyer snickered.

Wyatt turned and threw his arms around Sawyer's neck. "Hi!"

"Wow," Sawyer held his brother close. "I missed you, little shit." Sawyer smiled and pulled away from his brother. "We brought some guests. You remember Tucker and Wesley from the Denali pack?"

Wyatt smiled and hugged Tucker and Wesley, they had helped when Dakota had been kidnapped. They hadn't aged a day it seemed, but being a werewolf gave you a youthful appearance for a long time. His dad was in his fifties and didn't look a day over thirty. Wyatt's eyes met with his dad's. There was a smile there and Wyatt flew into his arms.

"I'm so sorry, Dad."

"It's okay, Wyatt, I'm just glad you learned a lesson. You *did* learn a lesson right?" John chuckled softly. He held his son in his arms and closed his eyes. Wyatt would always be his little boy.

"I did, Dad, I really did." Wyatt looked at all the firemen still dancing and his eyes met Preston's. Wyatt's senses picked up on arousal and he looked around trying to pinpoint it.

He heard a gasp and looked down the line of men. Tucker was watching one of the firemen and his hands were shaking by his sides.

Wyatt followed Tucker's line of sight but couldn't pinpoint anyone.

"Which one, Tucker?"

"I, I don't know, I can't tell, they are all so close together." Tucker tried to pinpoint the smell, it was damn arousing and he was getting hard.

"We'll figure it out. Come on guys, let's go mingle." Wyatt grabbed his dad's hand. "I want you to meet the guy I've fallen in love with, Dad."

John smiled. His son had found his mate and fallen in love. Preston had waited eleven years to be with Wyatt, waited patiently for him to be old enough and in the end, he had gotten him.

"I can't wait, son."

~~

Wyatt watched his family mingle with his new firehouse family. His father was in deep conversation with Preston and they seemed to be getting along. Olivia was sitting on Sean's lap drinking a soda and she winked at him when their eyes met. Once she had gotten past Big Red's shy demeanor he had opened up and had asked her out. She couldn't say yes fast enough. His brothers were all dancing with their husbands and Wyatt couldn't help but smile. Even though he had met his mate at the beach he considered Preston his true mate. Wyatt knew he would have to go back to the beach and try to explain to his mate that he'd fallen in love with someone else.

Wyatt made his way to Tucker and they watched all the firemen. Most of them had changed into their turnouts and walked around bare-chested for the women hanging around; he'd been informed that they did it once a year. Wyatt almost felt sorry for Tucker having to try and find the proverbial needle in a haystack. They made the rounds and Wyatt watched all his newfound brothers looking for some kind of sign as to which one was Tucker's mate. And then it was there. They'd made their way over to the keg and Wyatt saw Austin's skin break out in goose bumps, he shivered and turned around.

"Hey, Wyatt," Austin smiled at Wyatt and his friend. At first glance Austin could swear the guy had green eyes, now as he took a second

76

glance they were hazel, with gold exploding around the iris. The man was breathtaking and Austin felt his skin heating. "Um, who's your friend?"

Wyatt pushed Tucker forward and smiled when Austin licked his lips looking at Tucker.

"This is a friend of the family, Tucker Storm."

"Hey man, Austin Jacobson. It's nice to meet you." Austin put his hand out and Tucker shook it. Austin felt his cheeks heat. "Um, so where are you from?"

"I'll just be going now," Wyatt smiled at Austin and Tucker. If Austin wasn't gay he had a big surprise coming his way. Wyatt made his way over to Wesley; the guy was looking over the crowd in a slow sweep. "What's up?"

Wesley looked at Wyatt. "My mate is here, my skin is on fire." Wesley scanned the crowd. His eyes locked onto a fireman. "Shit," he whispered. "That's him."

"Where?" Wyatt looked in the direction Wesley was. "Oh, no."

"What?" Wesley looked at Wyatt. "What's wrong?"

"It's Kurt," Wyatt sighed. "He's so far from gay it's ridiculous."

"Of course he is," Wesley sighed.

Wyatt watched as Kurt raised an eyebrow and then to his surprise made his way over to him and Wesley.

"Wyatt, who's your friend?" Kurt smiled at the man.

"Um, this is Wesley Foster. Wes, this is Kurt Maguire."

"Nice to meet you," Wesley put his hand out and Kurt's enveloped it. The warmth from the touch sent a delicious tingle down his spine and Wesley could tell Kurt had been affected as well.

Kurt's body went up in flames. *What the fuck?* He tried to compose himself and smiled. "So, where are you from?"

"Well, I'll just let you two get acquainted," Wyatt winked.

Wyatt walked back to where Preston was and just stopped to look at him. He was smiling at something Xander was saying and his whole face lit up. Wyatt's heart rate went through the roof. His family liked Preston, everything was perfect. Wyatt walked over to Preston and slipped his arms around his neck. Preston's arms came around him and Wyatt relaxed into Preston. "How long do we have to stay here?" Wyatt whispered in Preston's ear.

"Why, Wyatt Quinton," Preston chuckled. "You little slut, you."

"Only with you," Wyatt looked into Preston's eyes. He swore he'd seen them before, knew he had but couldn't remember where. "Tucker found his mate - it's Austin."

"No shit?" Preston looked over at where Austin was engaged in conversation with Tucker.

"That's hilarious! Austin's straight, but looking at him now I don't think he's going to stay that way for long."

Wyatt felt the heat from Preston's body and it seeped into his bones making him melt in Preston's arms.

"Oh, and I think Kurt is Wesley's," Wyatt nuzzled Preston's neck. "I want to be alone with you."

Preston caressed Wyatt's face and leaned in pressing their foreheads together. "I was going to make you dinner tonight but I think we can skip that part. We've eaten enough here today."

"I didn't have dessert." Wyatt looked in Preston's eyes and licked his lips.

"Jesus, Wyatt," he whispered. "You have no idea how you make me feel."

"So, let's say our goodnights and go to your place. You do have a place right?"

"Yes, it's down by the university. Let's stay just a bit longer okay? I'm not going anywhere." Preston leaned in and kissed Wyatt's neck softly.

Wyatt heard the loud whistles and catcalls and looked up to see all the firefighters fanning themselves. "Oh, shut up."

Chapter Six

The party went into the evening hours and Preston watched Wyatt with his brothers Xander and Grayson. Taylor and Jagger had never looked so happy with their husbands and Preston finally knew how they felt. He had checked in on Wyatt over the years whenever he could. He had watched Wyatt go from a precocious seven year old to a man, and what a man he had become. Preston looked Wyatt over from head to toe. Wyatt's jeans clung to him, outlining his beautifully shaped ass and Preston wanted to grab it, knead it in his hands.

Jagger and Taylor were making their way over to him and he smiled when Tucker and Wesley fell in step with them. This was his pack. They had stayed together with Wayne as their alpha and Jagger as the beta. Preston moved over on the bench to give them room to sit down.

"So, are you guys enjoying yourselves?" Preston sat back and put his hands behind his head locking his fingers together.

Jagger looked over all the firemen. They didn't hold a candle to his mate. "When are you going to tell Wyatt you're his mate? You got what you wanted didn't you? He's obviously head over heels in love with you."

Preston sighed and smiled as Wyatt picked up one of the neighborhood kids and bounced the little boy on his knee. "I need to hear him say it and I don't want to say it first. I don't want him to say it because he feels he has to. God, I have waited so long to be with him and my fucking skin is on fire every time he touches me."

"Welcome to our world." Taylor smiled at his husband, Grayson, standing across the way with his family. "It took a lot to make it work but in the end I don't regret one damn thing. I love Grayson."

"I don't care what it takes, I love him. I always have. I finally got him away from Sebastian and I fully intend to keep him from now on." Preston watched Wyatt's biceps as he picked the little boy up and played airplane with him.

"Yeah, well he called Gray the other night and told him he had finally found his mate but when he asked him about *you* Gray said the way Wyatt talked about you it was like, 'mate who?'" Taylor playfully punched Preston in the arm.

"I'm going to be with him tonight and my whole body is screaming to take him and mark him. I have no idea how the hell I'm going to mask my scent or hide who I am from him if we get carried away. I've saved myself for him all this time. I can wait a little longer." Preston looked over at his pack. They all looked at him with their heads tilted. "What?"

"Yeah," Jagger snorted. "Good luck with that."

~~

Wyatt was so busy smiling at Preston he didn't notice his brothers staring at him until he felt the side of his face burning from Grayson's intense gaze. He turned to see Grayson's sly smile, the knowing look in his eye that Wyatt had known all too well growing up.

"I know, I know, yes I am in love with Preston."

"Duh," Grayson pulled Wyatt into a hug and held him close. He had missed his little brother. "Whatever happens, Wyatt, always trust your heart. It will never steer you wrong."

Xander got in on the hug, along with Sawyer.

"We love you." Xander mussed his brother's hair.

Preston made the rounds saying goodnight to everyone. Wyatt's father took him aside and Preston shook his hand and smiled at him. It had been hard on all of them to lie to Wyatt for so long about his mate. But it was what Preston had wanted since Wyatt had been so young.

"I want to thank you," Preston hugged John. "You raised one hell of a man, Mr. Quinton."

John smiled at Preston Dalton; he couldn't have asked for a better mate for Wyatt. "I believe you will be calling me Dad one day. He loves you, be happy."

~~

Preston had Wyatt in his Jeep bound for his apartment. His heart rate was through the roof as they pulled into the parking space in front of the apartment complex. Preston got out and went around the Jeep to help Wyatt out. He took his hand and they walked up the stairs to the second floor and Preston fumbled with his keys; he couldn't ever remember being this nervous. The key slid into the lock and Preston opened the door. "This is my home away from home."

Wyatt walked in and saw all the Native American art on the walls, the room had a cozy feel to it. The couch was a dark chocolate brown and looked like suede. A large plasma TV was on the wall and Wyatt smiled at all of Preston's movies on the shelf. The walls were painted tan with a stripe of blue to accent the colors of the furniture.

"I love it, it's so comfortable."

"Do you want a soda or something? I think I have some left." Preston opened the fridge and pulled out a soda and water. He turned to see Wyatt looking at his artwork on the wall.

"I picked those up over the years." Preston handed Wyatt the soda and opened the cap of his water. "I took tours of some of the reservations in

Washington and had to buy some of the art on sale. They just called to me." Preston looked at the picture of a black wolf in the snow, a white wolf sat next to it and they were both looking towards the full moon in the sky. "This one's my favorite."

Wyatt felt an ache in his heart. He turned to look at Preston and couldn't stop himself from caressing Preston's face. "I know I found my mate and I don't know if you really understand what that means, Preston. I'm supposed to want him above anyone else and yet here I stand in your apartment wanting you more than I have ever wanted anything in my life. I... I've never had sex, never let Sebastian touch me in that way, but when I look at you I want that and so much more. We barely know each other, and I don't want to scare you but I'm in love with you, Preston. I want you to make love to me. I want to feel your hands on me, kissing me, like I am the only thing that matters to you."

The confession had left him speechless. Preston knew his jaw was hanging open, everything he had ever wanted Wyatt to say had just spilled from his lips and Preston stood there like an idiot. Wyatt's face dropped and turned pink. Preston put his thoughts together and took Wyatt's hand. "I'm in love with you, too, Wyatt."

"You are?" Wyatt whispered.

"Yes, I am and I want to make love to you. I want to kiss you because you *are* the only thing that has ever mattered to me." And with that,

Preston took Wyatt in his arms and kissed him. The kiss turned desperate in seconds, both of them trying to undress the other, grabbing at clothing, zippers coming down and shirts flying off until they both stood in their boxers, still kissing. Preston picked Wyatt up and walked them to his room. He eased Wyatt onto the bed and looked at his gorgeous form. Well-defined abdominal muscles and a happy trail leading from his navel snuck under the waistband of his boxers. Wyatt's chest was heaving with excitement and Preston got on the bed and crawled up Wyatt's body, touching hot skin along the way.

"God, I want to taste every inch of you, Wyatt." Preston leaned in and kissed Wyatt's neck, running his tongue along the throbbing pulse and making his way to the sensitive collarbone, which he nibbled. He could hear Wyatt's soft whimpers as his tongue explored. "Tell me what you want, Wyatt."

Wyatt felt his body pulsing, his muscles tightening then relaxing under Preston's hands. He felt soft feather-light touches down his chest and soft caresses followed by a warm mouth and tongue. "I want," Preston's tongue ran over one of his nipples and Wyatt groaned. "Oh God, I want everything, I want it all." Wyatt tunneled his fingers through Preston's hair as the warm mouth licked and nibbled at each nipple, taking them in and sucking softly. Wyatt's eyes changed and his fangs exploded out of his gums.

"Oh shit," Wyatt panted.

Preston felt the muscles rippling under his hands and looked at Wyatt's face. His eyes were squeezed shut and the tips of his fangs could be seen under his top lip. Preston made his way back up Wyatt's chest licking and kissing a path back up to Wyatt's lips. His tongue played with Wyatt's fangs, sliding across and over them feeling the sharp tip on the end of his tongue. "That's so fucking sexy," Preston looked at Wyatt's face. Sweat beads popped up on his brow. "Open your eyes Wyatt. I want to see you, all of you."

"I'm wolfing out," Wyatt felt his fingers heating. "My fingers…oh God, Preston, I'm sorry."

Preston cupped Wyatt's dick and heard a loud gasp, Wyatt's eyes flew open and Preston saw Wyatt's lupine eyes staring back at him.

"My God, you are so beautiful." Preston had never wanted to make love to Wyatt more than he did right now. Wyatt was losing control of his lupine side and it turned Preston on beyond belief. Preston squeezed Wyatt's cock and heard a low growl emanating from him. "Oh fuck, yeah," Preston bit Wyatt's lip softly. "Do that again."

Wyatt lay there in shock. Preston loved that he was shifting? Most people would run away screaming. It had never happened with Sebastian, he had never lost control like he was right now. Wyatt felt the heat from Preston's hand on his dick and moved his hips to encourage more touch, more squeeze, more everything.

"Give me a reason to and I will," Wyatt leered.

Preston narrowed his eyes at Wyatt and smiled. "Why, you little shit." Preston kept his eyes on Wyatt's face as he hooked a finger under the waistband of Wyatt's boxers and pulled them down. Wyatt arched his back and Preston took them off the rest of the way and looked into Wyatt's eyes as his hand wrapped around Wyatt's hard prick. His hand was on fire almost immediately and Wyatt's muscles rippled on contact, he kept a slow stroke all while watching Wyatt's eyes. Wyatt's hips were moving into his hand keeping time with every stroke on his cock, his tongue moved inside Wyatt's mouth, keeping the tongue strokes in time.

Their breaths mingled and moans escaped from them both as Preston's hand worked Wyatt into a frenzy, twisting at the base of Wyatt's cock in an upward movement. When Preston felt Wyatt's dick pulse in his hand, he knew what he was going to do. In a flash he moved to Wyatt's pulsing prick and swallowed him whole. The loud growl reverberated throughout the whole apartment as Wyatt came in his mouth and Preston swallowed and kept swallowing as his mate's release washed over his tongue. The flavors invaded his senses and in that brief second, part of his lupine side came free. He heard Wyatt's loud gasp and looked up. "What?"

Wyatt hadn't realized his claws had extended and had punctured the mattress. He removed his hands from either side of the bed and watched as they became human fingers again. "What was that? I felt," Wyatt furrowed his brows. "I felt something just then."

"A mind blowing orgasm?" Preston smiled and bit the inside of Wyatt's thigh. He took a good long look at the prick that had been in his mouth and what a thing of beauty it was. Even partly soft it was more than average and thick. The perfect cut mushroom head glistened with Preston's spit and lingering cum was seeping from the slit. Preston gave it a chaste kiss before returning to Wyatt's mouth, allowing him to taste himself. Their tongues teased and tangled and Preston felt his cock leaking in his boxers; he was so fucking hard it hurt.

"I have to be honest. I've never done any of this before so grade me on a curve okay?"

Wyatt's eyes widened. "You mean you've never..."

"No," Preston blushed and closed his eyes with a loud sigh. "I've been waiting for the man I love."

"But you just...and it was....I mean...wow," Wyatt chuckled.

"Hours and hours of porn," Preston kissed Wyatt's shoulder softly, loving the taste of him. "I want to make love to you and I want it to be good for you. So whatever feels good, tell me and whatever doesn't, do the same okay?" Wyatt nodded and Preston reached over for the bottle of lube he kept hidden in his nightstand. He flipped the cap open and spread a generous amount on his fingers and around his cock from root to tip. Being a werewolf had its perks, you couldn't catch anything therefore you couldn't spread it either. Making love to Wyatt bare would take every ounce of control he had. Preston leaned over to kiss Wyatt as he slipped a finger over Wyatt's opening, he didn't breach the ring, just gave it a slow easy rub.

"How's that feel?"

Wyatt closed his eyes as Preston's tongue licked a path across his lips.

"Feels good, more."

A slight pressure and Wyatt could almost hear the 'pop' as the tip of Preston's finger breached the ring of muscles in his chute. A slight burn followed by a warm flush up his thighs had Wyatt begging for more. His breaths became more labored as Preston's finger moved up his tunnel twisting around; another finger and Wyatt's back arched off the bed. The kissing became more frenetic as Preston rubbed him into a slow, rolling boil and then the warmth was gone, replaced with a searing heat that had Wyatt crying out.

"P-Preston…"

"Tell me when to move and I will."
Preston's arms shook as he held himself in place,
not moving at all, his cock pressed into Wyatt up
to the crown and not an inch more. He waited what
seemed like hours but was really only seconds and
then Wyatt was moving, pushing himself down on
Preston's aching prick, desperate for more. Preston
moved inside Wyatt inch by agonizing inch until
his thighs were flush with Wyatt's ass. They
stayed motionless for a few heartbeats before
Preston drew back slowly, feeling every ridge and
pulse inside Wyatt. Long, drawn out moans
accompanied the in-stroke and Preston settled into
a slow rhythm, keeping his mouth fused to Wyatt's
as he made love for the first time in his life.

They were pressed together, anchored with
sweat and arms wrapped around each other. Their
bodies moved together, Wyatt meeting Preston's at
every stroke and Preston couldn't get enough.
Wyatt's hard prick was rubbing against his
stomach as he thrust in again and again and again.
The room was spinning and Preston's eyes were
shifting, he reeled it back in and felt his orgasm
building in his balls; Wyatt's moans and whimpers
were getting louder and Preston held out, waiting,
waiting for his mate to release all over both of
them - because God help him he wanted to come
inside Wyatt and mark him.

Preston's name left Wyatt's lips in by far the
loudest growl yet and Preston's lupine side was set
loose. He reared back and let out a growl of his

own, his dick shot hot spurts of ejaculate into Wyatt and before he could stop himself he collapsed on Wyatt and sunk his canines into Wyatt's shoulder. He came again and again and again as Wyatt's body shook and shuddered beneath him with his own release. Preston lay there for what seemed like forever waiting for Wyatt to call him out. It didn't happen. Slowly Preston drew out of Wyatt and looked into his face; he had passed out. Dried blood was caked on Wyatt's shoulder and Preston got up quietly and grabbed a washcloth from the bathroom. He cleaned Wyatt up and looked for any other evidence of what he had done, bruises were fading on Wyatt's body until they were completely gone and all the while Wyatt remained still, breathing soft and even.

Preston crawled back into bed and pulled Wyatt into his chest. He pulled the blankets up and caressed Wyatt's angelic face. Did he fuck Wyatt into a coma? Preston was starting to worry that he had hurt Wyatt somehow, but he was breathing so that meant he was okay. Didn't it? The panic started to rise in him until Wyatt mumbled his name with a soft sigh. He had finally taken Wyatt and made him his; Preston couldn't stop the rush of pride even if he wanted to. Wyatt was his, marked and claimed. If Wyatt called him on it when he woke up then so be it, he was Wyatt's mate and the call could not be denied. Even when Wyatt hadn't known that he himself was his mate,

Wyatt had fallen in love. Preston settled back on the bed and drew Wyatt close to him and kissed his forehead and lips softly.

"I love you, Wyatt Quinton," he whispered.

~~~

Wyatt woke up with a raging hard on and heat on his back. A warm hand was on his stomach in protective grip and Wyatt smiled. Preston. The night before had been everything he had ever wanted, the man he loved had made love to him and it had been worth the wait. Preston had been tender and caring, making sure that he was comfortable the whole time. Of course after his second, third and fourth mind-blowing orgasm he had passed out; his body couldn't take the pleasure overload and shut down. Wyatt turned his head to see Preston's beautiful face. The long blond eyelashes covered his gorgeous brown bedroom eyes. Wyatt's man was a walking wet dream. He smiled at that, because that wet dream was all his. Wyatt rolled over carefully, trying not to wake Preston. He wanted to stare at him while he slept. Wyatt chuckled. He was stalking his sleeping boyfriend. Wyatt smiled at the thought: Preston was his boyfriend. Or so he hoped.

"You're staring at me," Preston smiled keeping his eyes closed.

"I know, I can't help it, you're so beautiful." Wyatt traced Preston's lips with his fingertip. "I'm sorry I kinda checked out last night. I think my body shut down so I wouldn't shift and then you'd be making love to a wolf."

"Awesome," Preston chuckled and drew Wyatt closer to him, the heat from their bodies creating a warm cocoon in the bed.

Wyatt kissed Preston's neck and followed the rapid pulse up to his ear. "You were fantastic," he breathed into Preston's ear.

Preston shivered as Wyatt's lips brushed his ear seductively. "Although you have nothing to compare it to, I will take that as a compliment. You will be my first as well, Wyatt."

Wyatt felt his cheeks heating and hid in the crook of Preston's neck. "What if I can't, you know, please you?"

"I don't think that's possible, Wyatt," Preston pulled Wyatt on top of him and took Wyatt's face in his hands. "I don't think you could be bad at it, you are so full of passion." Preston brought Wyatt's lips to his own and gave him a slow sensual good morning kiss. Their hot breaths mingled as their lower bodies ground into each other; Preston wanted to go for round two already. "How about tonight I take you out to dinner and a movie and then we can meet the guys at the club?"

"Gay or straight club?"

Preston thought about it, it was Saturday which meant it would be straight night. "Straight, I owe Sean, but I think he'll have a date."

Wyatt laid his head on Preston's chest listening to his heartbeat. "Okay, will you tell me all about yourself at dinner? Where you were born, what your childhood was like?"

"I'll tell you anything you want to know, Wyatt, we are together now," Preston looked into Wyatt's eyes. "We are together, aren't we?"

Wyatt let out a sigh of relief. "I want to be."

"Then we are."

~~~

They spent the day together. Preston stopped in at the firehouse to do some checks and then they were off to the beach. They walked hand in hand and Preston watched Wyatt's face as he talked. Wyatt was so happy he actually glowed. Preston chewed his lip in thought; how was he going to tell Wyatt the truth about himself? How would he explain that he'd known since the age of thirteen that Wyatt was his? Since that fateful day of the meetings between packs, Preston had known little Wyatt was his. Even though Xander and Grayson had been right there with Wyatt, he'd known which one his mate was. It had never been in question. He'd realized it right there and then. When Carson had come for Dakota, Preston snuck in the back of the truck, found Wyatt in the woods and covered him with his own scent.

Even before he'd bent the rules of the pack, his life hadn't been easy. His parents had been cruel when he had come out, threatened to disown him unless he went to see a shrink. With Tucker and Wesley by his side they all left their homes and immersed themselves into pack life. They attended school and all three had graduated from high school and gone on to college. Although Preston understood the call of one's mate, after how his parents had treated him he needed to know without a doubt that Wyatt loved him for who he was, not just because they were mates. Preston was startled out of his thoughts by Wyatt's smooth sexy voice.

"Are you thinking about sex with me?" Wyatt grinned.

Preston chuckled and pulled Wyatt around to face him. "That's not all I want from you Wyatt." Preston's hand caressed Wyatt's face, the pad of his thumb moved over Wyatt's full lips. "I love everything about you, the way you smile, the way you laugh, the way your eyes light up." Preston leaned in to kiss Wyatt, his fingers caressing the side of Wyatt's neck in a gentle rhythm. He had never kissed anyone before Wyatt. He wanted Wyatt to be his first everything. Their lips flowed over one another and Preston sighed in Wyatt's mouth. Preston broke the kiss and looked into deep green pools; Wyatt's eyes were wet. "What is it?"

"I've never been kissed like that," Wyatt whispered. "It's like everything you're feeling is being transferred to me and it's so overwhelming with emotion." Wyatt took a deep breath and let it out slowly. "I can feel how much you love me." Wyatt looked up into Preston's eyes. "It's like we've known each other forever."

Preston smiled and took Wyatt's hand. They continued walking down the beach, arms swinging. "I feel the same way."

~~~

After stopping at the apartment to change, Preston took Wyatt to Palisade Restaurant on Elliot Bay. They sat in the corner bathed only in candlelight. Wyatt was drinking his sparkling cider while his eyes looked over Preston's body in his casual button up shirt. The biceps flexed with each and every tiny movement and Wyatt felt his dick getting hard just watching Preston twirl a breadstick between his fingers. When he looked up and met Preston's eyes he could see the desire within them. Wyatt swallowed hard and licked his lips nervously.

"So, um, where did you grow up?" Wyatt asked.

Preston sat back and bit into his breadstick. He chewed and smiled at Wyatt who was nervously playing with his fork. "I grew up in Sterling, Alaska. My dad was in the Air Force and when I came out at twelve," Preston shrugged. "Let's just say he was less than thrilled to have a fag for a son. I left, they never came looking. I and two other guys I hung out with took off to

Anchorage and we ran into some other guys who were kind of in the same boat. I finished school in Anchorage and went on to college. I sent my parents my diploma with a note that said," Preston lowered his voice and looked around the crowded restaurant, "I did it without you, assholes." Preston smiled thinking about it. "I spent so much time hating them for abandoning me, betraying me and then one day I just realized that I didn't care anymore. I could do everything on my own."

Wyatt smiled and took Preston's hand; his heart ached for him. He'd never had a problem coming out. Hell, his dad was blessed with four gay sons and hadn't even batted an eyelash. "I'm so sorry they were stupid. You have me now. You don't have to do anything on your own." Wyatt thought about Preston, alone in Alaska, with no one to love him or hold him and the anger grew inside him so fast he knocked his glass of water over. "Crap," Wyatt whispered. He took his napkin and tried to sop up the water on the tablecloth. He felt Preston's hand slide over his own and looked up.

"It's okay, it made me stronger, Wyatt, but you're right. I'm not alone anymore." Preston squeezed Wyatt's hand.

"Did you always want to be a firefighter?"

"Yes, my first toy was a fire truck. I played with it all the time. I used to make little fires and then put them out." Preston sat back thinking about the fire he had started in the back yard before he had been kicked out. It had gotten bigger than he had expected and he'd kept his cool and gotten it out before anyone knew it even started. Wyatt had been quiet and Preston looked up to see him smiling at him. "What?"

"My first toy was a fire truck, too," Wyatt smiled.

"Did you want to be a fireman?"

"I think I always did, because of what I am I could be of use you know? Lift stuff."

"Able to leap tall buildings in a single bound?" Preston smiled.

"Isn't that Batman?" Wyatt laughed softly.

Preston pointed at Wyatt with his breadstick. "That's Superman."

"Whatever," Wyatt laughed and sipped his cider. "Does it bother you that I'm younger?"

"Nope," Preston shook his head. "I love the fact that I have a young stud for a boyfriend."

Wyatt blushed and gave Preston his best seductive smile. "Well, I'll show you just how long I can last later."

Preston was mid-sip when he coughed, inhaling water. His eyes went wide as Wyatt's tongue did a slow sweep of his lips and then the breadstick was sliding in and out of his mouth. "Stop that." Preston looked around the restaurant. "Jesus, Wyatt." Preston grabbed at his dick trying to rearrange himself.

"So, movies?"

~~~

If Preston thought the restaurant was bad, the movie theatre was worse. They sat way in the back and their hands would bump each time they reached for the popcorn. After the fourth or fifth time Wyatt grabbed at his cock and then they were making out in the theatre, movie long forgotten. The armrest was in the way and they got tangled up in each other's limbs, pulling and grabbing at each other. Preston had never been so damn turned on his whole life. He was aware that they were moaning loudly and the movie wasn't covering their moans and sighs.

Finally Preston detached Wyatt from him and they continued their make-out fest in the car. Wyatt straddled him in the seat and Preston reclined it all the way back. The Jeep was rocking as Wyatt dry humped him. Their pants unbuttoned, Wyatt slid his dick over Preston's in a long, slow drag that had them both moaning. Preston had a grip on the roll bar and his knuckles turned white when Wyatt switched up the pace; in one quick movement Wyatt inched down Preston's body and started sucking on his cock.

"Holy shit!" Preston's hips bucked and the horn went off from Wyatt's ass hitting it. They both broke out in hilarious fits of laughter and Preston dragged Wyatt up to his mouth for a kiss. "How about we try that when we get home?"

Wyatt wiped his mouth, and smiled with a wink. "Okay."

Chapter Seven

The parking lot of the club was packed and Preston took Wyatt's hand as they entered the building. They were stopped by Jesse, one of the bouncers, and Preston smiled when Jesse gave him a knowing wink and waved them through. Sean was at the bar with Olivia and Austin. They all waved when Preston walked over to them holding Wyatt's hand. The music changed immediately as the DJ spotted them and Preston waved at him giving him the thumbs up.

Preston crooked his finger at Wyatt. "Let's go shake our asses."

Wyatt was pulled into Preston's embrace. Juvenile's "Back That Ass Up" played loud through the speakers and the lights were flashing red and white. The dance floor was packed and Wyatt leaned his back into Preston's chest; his arms wrapped around Preston's neck and Wyatt threaded his fingers together. Preston's hands ran down his sides and across his stomach. Wyatt felt a shiver run down his spine as Preston's fingers hooked into the loops on the front of his jeans. They moved to the beat and Wyatt ground his ass into Preston's hard cock.

The club faded away as Wyatt moved to the beat with Preston, he tilted his head and found Preston's warm lips waiting for him. Preston's hand moved under his shirt caressing his stomach and Wyatt groaned into Preston's mouth. Wyatt opened his mouth and Preston's tongue slid inside, they kissed slowly and Wyatt was ready to cum screaming on the dance floor. The music changed and Wyatt was brought out of his seduction with a start, more of the guys from the firehouse showed up and the DJ was playing their song.

The whole club was shouting, "Up in here!" as the firemen lined up to do their dance. Wyatt stood with Olivia watching the guys shake their hips. Preston watched him the whole time, his hips rolled in a slow circle as he flexed his biceps. Wyatt's cock was so hard he could have cut glass with it. He wanted to make love to Preston more than he wanted anything else. When the dance was over Preston jogged over and picked Wyatt up, kissing him.

"Did you like it?" Preston put Wyatt down and kissed his cheek.

"I loved it, I always do. You look so sexy when you do that."

"I'll give you a private show later," Preston waggled his eyebrows.

Just one look from Preston had Wyatt's dick screaming in his pants. How he could have ever thought Sebastian was the one for him was ridiculous. Wyatt threw his arms around Preston's neck and kissed him. "I want you to come home with me for my birthday, can you?"

Preston nodded and ran his fingers through Wyatt's hair. "You bet yer cute sweet ass."

~~

The table was filled with firemen and Olivia sat on Sean's lap. Wyatt was happy she had finally found someone. Sean was a good guy, respected women and wasn't the kind to stray; he was perfect. Wyatt sat next to Preston holding his hand. They were retelling the stories of Wyatt's first days at the firehouse. Wyatt made a face and pinched Preston's ass.

"You were so mean to me."

"It's because I cared what happened to you." Preston kissed Wyatt's forehead. Suddenly, Preston was pushed forward into Wyatt's chair, knocking him over. Within seconds there was a wall of firemen in front of Preston and Wyatt. Two men were sneering at Wyatt on the floor.

"This is the straight bar, didn't you get the memo?" one of them said.

Preston felt the anger rising and his muscles rippled, he pushed through the wall of firemen and shoved the asshole who had spoken with one hand. "Yeah it is. The gay bar's down the street. Make your way over there."

Preston saw Jesse making his way over and smiled at the two men. "Nice meeting you guys, have a nice night." Preston turned and extended his hand to Wyatt, pulling him up. "I think we need a drink guys, huh?" Preston stood in front of his

103

firemen brothers and tried to calm them down. "Come on guys, they aren't worth it." Preston heard the grunts from his guys and smiled; they were a family, loyal to the end. Preston helped Wyatt back into his chair and kissed his forehead. "I'll be right back, babe."

Wyatt sat at the table and smiled at Austin; he was nervously looking around. "What's wrong?"

Austin leaned into Wyatt's ear. "Is that Tucker guy gay?"

Wyatt smiled and took Austin's hand. "Yes he is, why?"

"He didn't hit on me or anything. I just got the impression that he was." Austin looked around and lowered his voice. "I'm kind of freaking out here."

"Why?"

"I," Austin peeked around again, "I got a little embarrassed when people thought he was my boyfriend. I didn't say anything mean, you know? Just that I was straight, but I think I might have hurt his feelings," Austin said.

"Look, one of my brother-in-law's best friends was straight. He only had sex with women. It only took one look at my Uncle Mark and he was in love," Wyatt smiled. Josh was Sam's best friend and Wyatt had gotten into the habit of calling them all 'uncle.' "So it can happen you know? The right guy comes along and you never knew you could be attracted to a man and then you are. We're all human, Austin. Don't stop hanging out with him if you truly enjoy his company, what other people assume isn't your problem."

"Does it ever bother you? The things people say, the names they call you?" Austin asked.

Wyatt looked at Preston coming back with a drink and he felt his heart pounding. "No, because once you find the other half of yourself, nothing bothers you anymore. It's just words from people who are too closed minded to see that love exists no matter who you are or what sex you are."

"Thanks, Wyatt," Austin blushed. "I think I'll call Tucker then, he asked if I wanted to go see a movie sometime and I said I'd get back to him. He was real nice about it, too, said he'd understand if that felt weird."

"Just give it a chance, if nothing else you'll end up with a really good friend," Wyatt smiled as Preston came back and pulled him into his lap. "How did it go at the bar?"

"Easy, we come here all the time. I don't know who they thought they were," Preston chuckled and kissed Wyatt's nose.

"I want to go home, can we?"

Preston saw that look in Wyatt's eyes and knew it meant his engines were revving up. His cock was hard in seconds. "Yup."

~~~

The front door slammed into the wall as Preston entered the apartment with Wyatt, he kicked it shut all while keeping his lips firmly planted on his mate's. Their clothes were being discarded and Preston was tripping all while hopping down the hallway, one pant leg down, one shoe off. They landed on the bed in a tangle of limbs desperately trying to get their remaining clothing off.

Wyatt's lips and tongue were all over him and Preston white knuckled the comforter as Wyatt's teeth bit his hip bone. "Oh fuck….Wyatt…" Warm hands slid up his sides leaving goose bumps behind and then Preston felt Wyatt's mouth on his cock. His hips arched and he moaned, trying to keep his lupine side in check. Long licks and a twirling tongue had Preston breathing like he had run a marathon. Wyatt was licking his dick like an ice cream cone.

"I want you to cum in my mouth." Wyatt kept his eyes on Preston as his tongue slid up the length of Preston's engorged cock. It was a good-sized dick. Wyatt tried to figure out how he was going to fit it all in his mouth. He had no idea what he was doing. He tried to do what he'd seen in porn movies, he gripped the base and stroked, while his mouth sucked on the leaking tip. A hot, salty flavor tantalized his taste buds and Wyatt sucked harder trying to get out more of the taste he was craving. Preston's hips were bucking and Wyatt felt the dick in his mouth pulsing. He closed his eyes and sucked harder, stroking faster. The burst of flavor hit his tongue and he groaned taking in Preston's release; it flowed over his tongue sending a sensation straight to his cock. Wyatt grabbed the lube and covered his fingers and cock with it. He leaned over and looked into Preston's wide eyes. "Ready?"

"Uh huh," Preston licked his lips and Wyatt's mouth covered his. Wyatt devoured him as his fingers breached his chute. The warmth was immediate and his spine tingled as Wyatt's fingers stretched him, rubbed him in the spot that made his fingers grip the comforter and his ass clench around the fingers. Preston could sense Wyatt's hesitation and arousal at the same time. He opened his eyes and looked at Wyatt's lupine eyes. "Make love to me, Wyatt," he whispered.

"You sure?" Wyatt held the base of his cock at Preston's opening. Preston nodded and Wyatt lined himself up and pushed in to the crown. Preston's eyes went wide and Wyatt stopped and waited. The urge to cum hit so strongly that Wyatt started reciting the alphabet in his head. A voice broke through his alphabet; Preston's voice was in his head. Wyatt's brow furrowed and he heard it again. *Oh my God, oh my God.* Wyatt's eyes flew open and he looked at Preston on the bed, his eyes were closed and his breathing was uneven. "Did you say something?"

Preston blinked. *Oh shit.* "Yes, I said 'oh my God.'"

Wyatt smiled and pushed in slowly. His back was rippling, the muscles tensing, ready to shift and Wyatt took a deep breath and reeled it back. Preston's ass was warm and inviting. Wyatt slid in like butter, his thighs were flush with Preston's and he leaned over and ran his tongue across Preston's lips. Their mouths opened and they settled into a lazy sensual kiss as Wyatt drew back slowly. He was making love for the first time in his life and he wanted it to last forever. Well, longer than five seconds. Each in-stroke had his arms shaking and Preston moaning, the heat surrounding his cock was like nothing he'd ever felt before. Being inside Preston was an experience he would never forget. They moved together perfectly, they were meant to be and Wyatt knew it.

"God, this feels so good, Preston, you feel so fucking good," Wyatt moaned and Preston's legs came up and wrapped around his waist.

"Faster," Preston looked into Wyatt's eyes as they moved together, Preston meeting Wyatt's deep thrusts. The kisses became more desperate with each wanting to devour the other. The room temperature was climbing as Wyatt hit him with piston-fast strokes, his legs shook and his dick jumped on his stomach. Preston grabbed his leaking prick and groaned in Wyatt's mouth. "Oh God, I'm coming……I'm coming, Wyatt…" A loud growl filled the room and Preston's cock exploded with so much force it hit his chin and the headboard above him.

Wyatt's spine snapped, his balls drew up impossibly high and his canines exploded through his gums; his eyes shifted and claws exploded through his fingertips. Preston's name left his lips in a long drawn out cry and he emptied himself in quick jerks into Preston. Wyatt collapsed. His canines were mere inches from Preston's flesh; he jerked away and flew off the bed into the wall. "Oh shit, oh shit…I can't stop it!" In the blink of an eye, Wyatt shifted.

Preston sat up in bed and looked at the large black wolf panting on his floor. He smiled and patted the bed next to him. "Come here, sexy." Wyatt whined and jumped on the bed settling into Preston's side. Preston stroked the soft black fur and lay down next to Wyatt hugging him in close. "You are so beautiful, Wyatt." Preston heard a soft snort and a low whine and he kissed Wyatt's head. "I love you, Wyatt Quinton."

~~*~~

Wyatt woke up seeing in color; he sighed and felt the warmth of Preston on his back. He had completely lost it last night and shifted after his amazing orgasm. Great, he might as well have humped Preston's leg. What the fuck was that? He had almost bitten Preston. Wyatt sighed and rolled over hiding his face in Preston's warm neck; his pulse was beating slowly and Wyatt could hear Preston's heart thumping in his chest. Wyatt wiggled his nose, everything was more magnified somehow. His skin buzzed with energy and his cock filled in seconds flat, what the hell was going on? He could hear a soft voice in his head, he pulled away slightly looking at Preston's face. Carefully, he ran his fingertips over Preston's warm lips and heard a soft moan. Wyatt smiled and leaned in kissing Preston's lips and nibbled on the bottom one gently.

"I could get used to this," Preston sighed and opened his eyes.

"A wolf fetching your paper? Maybe even your slippers?" Wyatt snickered and snuggled into Preston's side.

"You are beautiful in either form." Preston pulled Wyatt on top of him and grabbed Wyatt's firm ass in his hands.

Wyatt let out a slow breath. "I thought maybe I had freaked you out or something, I don't know what the hell happened. I couldn't stop it."

Preston took Wyatt's face and cupped it in both hands. "I loved every second of last night. I loved the fact that I got to see you in wolf form, Wyatt, and I would love nothing more than to wake up to you every morning and go to bed with you every night."

"Really?" Wyatt searched Preston's eyes.

"Why does that surprise you? I told you I loved you, Wyatt; I want a relationship with you." Preston pressed his hips into Wyatt's.

"It seems like you want something else, too," Wyatt chuckled as Preston flipped them over again. Preston's hips ground into his own and Wyatt closed his eyes at the delicious friction. "Don't you have to go into work?"

Preston sighed and shot a look at the clock. "Ugh, yeah I do; three on and three off." Preston lifted himself off of Wyatt and settled onto his elbow tracing the ridge of Wyatt's pectoral muscle. "I know we leave for the reservation in a few days but I was hoping you'd come stay with me at the firehouse anyway."

"Do I have to wash the hell bitch?" Wyatt smiled as Preston's tongue licked a path across his chest.

"Nope, but I'd love it if you'd cook." Preston smiled at the loud sigh emitted from Wyatt. "No pressure, we just like the way you cook."

"All right, it's a deal."

~~

The next three days flew by and Wyatt hardly saw Preston at all except when Preston fell into bed exhausted and wet from a shower. The alarm seemed to go off every time they were getting close to each other. Over those three days Wyatt had been reading Austin's firefighter test booklet. He read it from front to back and then back again. Walking around the firehouse, he picked out equipment that now had a name. On the last day Wyatt was eagerly awaiting Preston's shift to be over and decided to help Austin, who had gone back to being picked on. Wyatt helped him wash hell bitch while the guys slept off their long night. Austin whistled as he washed the side of the truck and Wyatt gave him a knowing glance. Austin blushed and pursed his lips together.

"Stop looking at me like that, Wyatt."

Wyatt feigned innocence. "Like what?"

"Like you know some deep, dark secret," Austin sighed and wrung out the sponge he was using.

"Did you go to the movies with Tucker?"

"Yeah, he was really sweet about it, too. Paid my way and bought me popcorn and a soda. He didn't try to hold my hand or anything. We just sat and watched this high action dude flick and then talked about it over drinks at Cuffs & Stuff Club."

Wyatt looked up, eyes wide. "You went to a gay bar with him?"

"I go all the time with you guys. It's never bothered me before. This is Seattle you know? I grew up in Montana. You think they have gay bars there?" Austin laughed loud. "The first time I called my parents and told them I'd gone clubbing at a gay bar they thought everyone was happy. They don't say 'gay' they say 'homosexual;' I don't even think they know the word 'gay'."

Wyatt bent over and clutched at his stomach laughing. "Stop it, you're killing me."

Austin leaned against the truck with a grin. "You should have seen the guys hitting on him, and he would just smile and say no and his attention was on me the whole night. I felt special, you know? No chick has ever been like that with me. It was like he only saw me." Austin saw Wyatt's smile. "Oh, cut it out."

"What?"

"I…I almost wanted to kiss him goodnight, but he just shook my hand and smiled, saying he'd call me some time to go out again. I felt like the girl in the whole scenario. It was freaky," Austin laughed.

Wyatt smiled at the dazed look on Austin's face. Tucker knew what he was doing; as Austin's mate he'd have to work carefully to secure Austin's trust which meant not trying to kiss him or touch him unless Austin initiated the act.

"Well he seems to really like you, he stayed by you the whole barbeque and never once did I see his eyes stray towards any of the other guys."

"Well I wouldn't be surprised if they did. Sean and Preston pretty much make me look like the ugly duckling."

Wyatt laughed and looked at Austin. "Seriously? You have beautiful eyes and a body that goes on for days. Tucker's a lucky guy," Wyatt winked. The ceiling woman spat and the alarms went off in the house. Wyatt sighed and backed away from the truck. "And here we go." Wyatt watched all the men flying down from the floor above; Preston jogged over to him and kissed him hard and quick.

"I'll be back," Preston winked.

"You better." Wyatt watched them all load up and the truck roared to life. He put the sponge back in the bucket and looked at the time. "Hey, Austin - I'll be back, okay? If Preston's back before me just tell him I went to eat crow."

~~

Wyatt pulled into the student parking lot at the University of Washington and closed and remote locked his truck. The walk to the dean's office suddenly felt like miles and Wyatt felt as if he was doing the walk of shame. He *should* be ashamed, he thought bitterly. Making his way past the teacher's lounge, he stepped into the dean's outer office where a secretary looked up and smiled at him. Wyatt read the nameplate and tried to smile.

"Um, hi, Mrs. Forbes, I'm here to see Dean Smith." Wyatt shuffled his sneakers on the carpet.

"Go right on in."

Wyatt took a deep breath and turned the knob to the office door; the glass was frosted on the door and Wyatt saw the dean's name in black lettering. He knocked anyway and heard a soft 'Come in.' Wyatt pushed through and stood at the front of the dean's desk. The baseball was on his desk, now in a small glass box. Wyatt closed his eyes and swallowed hard.

"I just wanted to come here and apologize in person for what I did. It was stupid and cruel and I should have never taken something that didn't belong to me." Wyatt saw Dean Smith motion to the chair and he sat down, clasping at his hands.

"Look, Wyatt," Dean Smith smiled. "I know this wasn't your brilliant idea, that's why I didn't press charges. Sebastian is angry with me because I put him on academic probation."

"You did?"

"Yes, his grades are failing and he won't be playing football next year if they continue to decline. He's in danger of losing his scholarship as well if he doesn't bring his GPA back up."

"I would have come sooner...I just..."

"I know - you were working down at the fire department." Dean Smith looked at Wyatt's flushed face. "You are a good kid, Wyatt, with a very bright future. Please don't let Sebastian Price drag you down with him." Dean Smith stood and extended his hand. "I look forward to seeing you in August, Wyatt, both in class and on the field."

Wyatt stood and shook Dean Smith's hand. "Thank you, sir."

Wyatt left the dean's office smiling. He had never felt better in his life. He crossed campus to his dorm room and packed a few things into a bag for the trip out to the Queets reservation. His skin was prickling just thinking about being alone with Preston. Stepping out into the abandoned hallway, Wyatt locked his room door and made his way down to the commons. Sebastian's smell invaded his senses.

"Sebastian..."

"Where are you off to?" Sebastian leaned against the wall and looked at Wyatt.

"Home, for my birthday," Wyatt threw his bag over his shoulder. "Have a good summer, Sebastian." Wyatt left before anything else could be said. He didn't want Sebastian to ruin his good mood.

Stepping out into the warm Seattle air he crossed the parking lot whistling a happy tune. He was going home to see his family, with Preston Dalton by his side. Halfway home, he realized he'd never gone back to the beach. Wyatt gripped the steering wheel; he couldn't put this off any longer. Pulling into the parking lot, he walked down to the sand of Alki beach and sat down to watch all the kids play. It would get dark soon, and he hoped that when he sent the message, his mate would hear it.

Why had this happened to him? As far as he knew, when you got your mate that was it. So why had he finally gotten his, but wanted Preston? Wyatt rubbed his face with his hands. What would he say to his mate? Oops, sorry, I found another guy? Wyatt closed his eyes thinking about the day his mate had protected him. The beautiful white wolf with brown eyes had covered Wyatt's scent from the evil Carson Drake. He'd never forgotten him and had always wondered what his human side looked like. Would he be tall? Would his hair be blond? He knew his mate had brown eyes, like liquid milk chocolate. The beach was clearing out as parents bundled their children in towels and grabbed their umbrellas. The sunset kissed the water and Wyatt took a deep breath, sending a message he hoped his mate would hear…

~~

Preston jumped from the fire truck and strode over to the benches. Dropping his helmet on the bench, he stopped and stiffened. Wyatt was calling to him, he sounded so …sad. Preston felt his body shiver with Wyatt's voice sliding down his spine. The urge to answer him was strong. Wyatt wanted him to come to him; he wanted to talk to him. Preston sighed, collapsing on the bench. He raised his head as Austin came in.

"Hey, Wyatt said he had to eat crow?" Austin said.

Preston nodded. "Thanks." Preston put his face in his hands. Wyatt's voice was insistent, calling to him to answer. He couldn't do it, it was cruel. He was going to have to tell Wyatt the truth, the faster the better. The despair and guilt wracked him, not only from Wyatt but himself. He had done what he'd had to do, hadn't he? He'd had this argument so many times with himself, it was ridiculous. When Preston realized that Wyatt was his mate, Wyatt was younger - a *lot* younger. He'd been a child. The mate bond, when it collided, meant sex and biting ... how the hell was he supposed to have contained himself when Wyatt was sixteen? He would have wanted to make love to him; he *had* wanted to make love to him, because Wyatt at sixteen had been breathtaking. Wyatt was just breathtaking at any age. Preston leaned over as Wyatt's voice became louder, begging him to come.

"Preston, man, what's going on?" Sean sat down next to Preston and rubbed circles on his back.

"Not here," Preston motioned upstairs.

Sean followed Preston up to the roof and closed the door behind them. He walked to the edge of the building where Preston was already sitting down, his feet dangling over the side. Sean sat down and looked up at the sky.

"It's Wyatt, isn't it?" Sean asked.

Preston nodded. "He's at the beach right now, asking me to come and talk to him. I can't, Sean. It's too cruel to keep the charade going."

"When are you going to tell him?"

"When we go to the reservation. I have no reason to keep it from him anymore and I want to do it on his home territory," Preston sighed. "He's so sad, he wants to explain himself. I can feel it."

"Why not just go then? Shift and let him see you?"

"I want to, trust me. But I think it's a bad idea. When I tell him, I want his family to be there as well. He needs to understand why we all kept our bond from him. They have that right. John and I agreed that Wyatt was too young when we first figured out I was Wyatt's mate. He wouldn't have been able to concentrate on anything but me. I don't know how many times this has happened before, with one of the mates being so much younger. Wayne said he'd look into it, but it doesn't matter anyway. I made the decision to stay away."

"But you didn't. You saw him, he just didn't see you," Sean raised a brow.

"I had to; it hurt my heart to be away from him."

Sean sighed, trying to smile. "I think you should tell him, the faster the better. Wyatt's headstrong and stubborn, Preston. How would you feel if the roles were reversed?"

Preston furrowed his brows. "Oh no…"

Sean nodded. "Oh, yeah."

Chapter Eight

Morning found Wyatt in Preston's Jeep flying down I-5. Wyatt relaxed into the heated seat; the music was blasting on the stereo and Wyatt sang along. The crisp morning air whipped his short hair and he watched the towns fly by. They passed through Olympia and hooked up with the 8. Wyatt watched as the scenery changed; the road became two lanes and Mountain Hemlock trees towered, reaching towards the sky. Wyatt let the sights and sounds invade his senses, he could almost taste the ocean. His mate had never answered him the night before, and Wyatt felt as if somehow he'd known that would happen. He was going to try again when they got back. His mate deserved that. The three hour drive seemed to fly by and before he knew it Preston was pulling onto the reservation. Wyatt saw his dad come out with his brothers and jumped out of the Jeep.

"Dad!" Wyatt flew into his father and hugged him, closing his eyes.

"Whoa!" John smiled, holding his son. "Look at you, seems like just yesterday you stood up to my kneecaps."

"I missed you, Dad." Wyatt opened his eyes to see Joe and Nadine coming out of their house. "Hi Nadine, Joe!"

"Look at you, little Wyatt Quinton," Nadine smiled and watched Preston making his way over. "And you brought a friend."

"Oh! Yeah. Nadine. Joe. This is Preston, my boyfriend." Wyatt could feel his cheeks warming.

Nadine smiled and took Preston's hand with a wink. "It's good to meet you, Preston."

"Well," John looked at Wyatt and Preston. "Let's get you two settled and then we can all eat lunch."

Wyatt looked around. "Where are Dakota and Sam?"

"Everybody's coming. They will all be here tonight when we have the bonfire." John took his son's hand. "Now come with me so I can get you and Preston settled in."

The rest of the afternoon was spent with Wyatt showing Preston the reservation. They walked along the shoreline taking in the sun and the smell of the water. Wyatt told Preston all about growing up on the reservation. They walked hand in hand and Wyatt smiled up at the man he was in love with. By the time they got back, Nadine had made dinner and everyone had shown up. Grayson and Xander sat with their husbands, along with Sawyer and Troy on one side of the large wooden table. Wyatt smiled at Dakota and Sam next to him. Dakota took his hand and kissed his forehead.

"Sam and I got you a gift." Dakota handed the box to Wyatt with a grin.

"That's sweet, guys." Wyatt opened the box and looked inside. He laughed and pulled out the babble ball he had enjoyed so much as a pup. "No way!"

121

"Yep, we even put batteries in it," Sam chuckled softly.

Wyatt shook the ball and the helium voice spat out of it. *'Good doggie.'*

"This is cool guys," Wyatt hugged Dakota. "I love it. I love *all* of the gifts." Wyatt grinned at his father.

"What? If you insist on wearing an earring, it should be an emerald."

"Okay, now for the cake!" Nadine clapped her hands together.

"Guys," Wyatt smiled at the table full of people and felt Preston's hand on his thigh. "This is so sweet. You didn't have to do all of this for me. Nineteen is not a milestone."

"It is to us." John squeezed his son's shoulders. Nadine brought the cake out and set it in front of Wyatt. John kissed Wyatt's head. "Make a wish."

"Okay." Wyatt closed his eyes and thought of Preston. He wished they would be together forever. Wyatt took a deep breath and blew out all the candles. The table erupted in clapping and Wyatt swiped at the icing on the side of the cake. He looked at Nadine, eyes wide. "Rum?"

"It's your birthday," Nadine shrugged.

Laughter filled the house as they all took turns talking about Wyatt's childhood. The group made their way out to the bonfire with cups of coffee and sat down on the variously sized stumps that doubled as seats. Wyatt was pulled into

Preston's lap and he nestled into his boyfriend's warm body as Archer took his spot in front of the group. Stories of shape shifters were told, stories of their heritage that Wyatt had never bothered to learn.

Hours had passed and Wyatt yawned, feeling Preston's warm body beneath him. Wrapped in a cocoon of warmth, Wyatt closed his eyes as talk flowed around the fire. When he opened his eyes he was in Preston's arms and they were walking to Wyatt's house. The fire was being put out behind them and Wyatt fell back into a state of perfect relaxation. He felt his body being lowered and then his shoes coming off. Wyatt rolled over and grabbed at a soft pillow burying his face in it. Warm lips touched his and he moaned softly. "Nite," Wyatt sighed.

"Night, baby," Preston brushed a strand of hair from Wyatt's forehead. "I love you."

~~

The white wolf was running next to him, they played in the water and wrestled on the white sand. The sun high in the sky, Wyatt rolled over his mate and nuzzled his neck, whining. The white wolf stood tall looking at him; beautiful brown eyes conveyed so much. "I love you, Wyatt."

Wyatt sat up in bed breathing hard. He looked at the time - nine in the morning. Wyatt stood up and stretched; he grabbed his socks and tiptoed down the hall to Xander's old room. Preston was asleep on his stomach, one leg stuck out from under the heavy down comforter. Wyatt sat on the edge of the bed and stared at Preston's back. The tattoo of the wolf was in full view and Wyatt looked closer. He gasped. The tattoo was of him in wolf form. The black wolf with green eyes was him. Wyatt stood up and left the room quietly. He went to the kitchen and grabbed a coffee cup. The coffeemaker was percolating and Wyatt grabbed it mid-brew. He left the house quietly and stood outside looking at the sky. Why did Preston have a tattoo of him on his shoulder?

Wyatt sat down on the front steps of the porch and took a deep breath. His nose caught Sebastian's scent before he saw him. Wyatt stood up and walked towards the fire pit; Sebastian was seated on a stump smiling at him.

"What part of 'it's over' did you not understand, Sebastian?" Wyatt set his coffee cup down on one of the other stumps.

Sebastian stood and looked at Wyatt. "I thought I said it was over when *I* said so."

"Go away, Sebastian, and don't come back." Wyatt turned to go back to the house; anger suddenly filled his senses and he turned in time to catch Sebastian's fist before it hit his face. He held it firmly, applying pressure on the knuckles. "I don't want to hurt you, Sebastian, but I will if you don't stop."

"Son of a bitch!"

Wyatt turned to look for Preston but he wasn't there. Wyatt's brows knitted. He'd heard Preston, he knew that for sure. Preston's voice was loud and clear in his head and yet Preston was nowhere to be seen. It hit Wyatt like a wrecking ball and he gasped. "Oh God; it's Preston."

"What's Preston?" Sebastian was trying to get his hand loose. A white wolf emerged from between the houses and Sebastian's jaw dropped. "Uh, can you let go now?"

Wyatt let go and Sebastian made a run for his car. Wyatt turned to look at Preston and saw him backing away. "Oh, no you don't!"

Wyatt walked over to him and knelt down. "Don't you dare, Preston! You have a hell of a lot of explaining to do!" Wyatt's face was nuzzled by a cold nose and then a soft whimper. "Stop trying to butter me up and go shift back." Wyatt waited impatiently for Preston to return. He finally came out in faded blue jeans and a firehouse T-shirt.

"Why, Preston? Just tell me why."

"I...I knew you were my mate when I was thirteen, Wyatt." Preston stopped and waited for the information to sink in. "You were *seven* at the time and I knew I couldn't make you mine then. So I waited, I kept tabs on you, watched you over the years and when you turned eighteen I went to tell you who I was. Imagine my surprise when my mate was in the arms of another man," Preston sighed and sat down on the front porch. "There

125

were so many times I wanted to tell you who I was, but I wanted you to love me, Wyatt, for me, not just because we were fated to be together."

"All this time," Wyatt shook his head. "Everyone told me I was crazy. That I made the whole thing up, that my mate – you - didn't exist and it was all in my head. I actually thought for the longest time that I was crazy and now I find out that not only do you exist, but I'm already in love with you." Wyatt looked at Preston. "You all lied to me. Did you get a good laugh at my expense?"

"It wasn't like that, Wyatt! I was six years older, hell, you didn't know what having a mate entailed and there was no way in hell I was going to stick around through my teen years being attracted to a kid six years younger than me! Don't you get it, Wyatt? I had to wait for you. I didn't have a choice!"

"Everyone has a choice, Preston. You chose wrong." Wyatt turned to go back to the house.

"I wanted you to love me, Wyatt, without knowing why."

Wyatt turned to look at Preston. "Well congratulations, you succeeded."

Preston watched as Wyatt shifted and ran for the forest. He contemplated running after him and in the end sat down and buried his face in his hands.

~~~

Stupid! I was so stupid! Wyatt ran through the forest as fast as his four legs would take him. He swung to the right and hit the beach, running through the water. His head pounded with the pack trying to breach his mind. *No.* He would not talk to them. For eleven years Preston was his mate and kept the truth from him for eleven fucking years. His whole family knew and acted like Wyatt was crazy for even thinking he'd found his mate. He'd never forget that day in the forest. The bad men came and took Dakota, and Wyatt watched as they loaded Dakota into a truck. Then he was picked up carefully between long canines and moved down the hill.

That was when the white wolf had masked Wyatt's scent with his own, Preston's scent. Wyatt ran back into the forest on the other side of the beach and hoped he had covered his tracks. He didn't want to be found, didn't want to hear the excuses of the people he thought loved him. Where would he go now? Home? Back to the dorms? The pain of betrayal and lies invaded him and if he was in human form he would have been bawling. He was in love with Preston and that would never change. Wyatt skidded to a stop and let out a loud, devastated howl.

~~~

Preston sat on the roof of the firehouse watching life go on. Two weeks. Two weeks gone without a word from Wyatt, either aloud or mentally. His heart hurt and he couldn't breathe. The separation was crushing him and Preston could barely get up out of bed. He talked to John almost every day hoping to hear that they had heard from Wyatt; so far, not one word. Even Olivia searched for Wyatt. She was blowing up his phone on a daily basis. Preston sighed and closed his eyes, bringing forth an image of Wyatt: his green eyes, his smile, his laugh. Preston could hear the people below on Main Street laughing, going about their day. Couples having coffee at the tables in Occidental Park; life was going on for them. His life was in shambles.

"Preston," Sean coughed quietly. "Dude, you have to try—"

"Try to what, Sean? Get over it?" Preston shook his head sadly. "Not going to happen. Wyatt is my mate and you will never understand what that means. I can't breathe without him, don't you get that?"

"But you were good before, what the fuck changed?"

"I marked him, made him mine." Preston saw the confusion in Sean's eyes. "I made love to him and then I bit him. I sealed our bond."

Sean sat down on the concrete and hung his legs over the side of the building. "I didn't know how all that shit went down. So that makes a big difference?"

Preston moved next to Sean and looked at the people below. "Yes, he's mine," Preston sighed and lie back looking at the sky. Clouds were forming, gray ugly-looking rain clouds. "It's going to come down on us tonight."

They both heard a soft cough and turned to see Austin shuffling his feet.

"Um, hey guys." Austin ran his hand through his hair and gave them a lopsided grin. "S'okay if I sit with ya?"

Preston nodded to the open rooftop. "Pick a spot. How's Tucker?"

Austin smiled and blushed. "He's good. We've gone out to dinner and the movies. I took him out to the cops versus firefighters football game. He was shouting and stuff and totally into it, I didn't even know…" Austin blushed again and averted his eyes.

"That gays liked football?" Preston watched Austin's reaction and smiled. "We do, and we like hockey, too, the tighter the pants the better." Preston tilted his head. "Did he tell you what he does for a living?"

"He wanted to know all about me, where I grew up, where I went to college," Austin blinked in surprise. "We never did talk about what he does. What does he do?"

129

Preston smiled wickedly. "He's a cop, Austin."

"No shit?" Austin shivered. "Wow, that's kind of hot."

"Well, seems like the cop has the hots for the fireman," Preston winked.

Austin cracked up. "The way he looks at me, you know? I've never had a chick look at me the way he does," Austin sighed and looked out over Main Street. "He doesn't hold my hand or try to kiss me, either. He's just real sweet to me." Austin realized he was talking out loud and looked at Preston and Sean smiling at him. "Knock it off."

"Hey if this guy lights your flame dude," Sean shrugged his shoulders. "You know how the guys in the house are. They don't give a shit that Preston's gay."

"That's because you threatened to step on them," Preston laughed and rolled out of Sean's reach. "How's Olivia, huh, Big Red? Has she seen your Big Red?" Preston yelped at the punch to his arm from Sean.

"A gentleman never kisses and tells." Sean crossed his arms over his chest.

"So there *has* been kissing!" Austin puckered his lips.

Sean smacked Austin's lips with the back of his hand. "Shut up, probie."

"Damn," Preston took a deep breath. "Can you smell the gyros? Who's making a run to Main?"

Preston and Sean both looked at Austin.

"Fine," Austin threw his hands up in the air. "As long as I don't have to wash the hell bitch." Austin saw Preston's face fall and immediately kicked himself. "Aw man, I'm sorry."

"No, it's okay," Preston sighed and stood up.

The alarms went off and all three men sighed.

"Time to save some lives," Preston put his arms around Sean's and Austin's shoulders. "Think we can get the gyros to go?"

~~~~

Wyatt rolled over on his side and flipped through channels on the TV. Nothing good was on, thousands of channels and nothing was on. Wyatt sighed and flipped on his back, hanging his head off the side of the bed and watching TV upside down. His dad had brought him back to the dorms and Wyatt said he would call. He didn't. Anger led him now and he couldn't see past it. He shut off his scent and his ability to communicate with the pack. The first week back was spent running at night. He went to Wenatchee and just ran. Ran to forget, ran to lessen the hurt. He dodged Olivia and Sean as much as possible. He didn't want to hear it. The rest of the pack was constantly trying to communicate with him and Wyatt kept himself shut off.

Now he was camped out in his dorm room watching TV and eating popcorn. He missed Preston, his hands, his lips, his eyes. Wyatt sighed and looked at the time. Preston would be at work. The worst part? He knew Preston was right. He wouldn't have been able to concentrate on anything else but Preston had he known. Didn't mean he wanted to admit to it. The knock on his door startled him and he sat straight up on the bed. Sebastian. Fuck.

"Open up, Wyatt." Sebastian knocked on the door.

"Go away." Wyatt flopped back down and put a pillow over his head.

"I'm not leaving until you open up."

Wyatt threw his pillow at the door. "Why can't you all just leave me alone?"

"Who are you all? I'm just here to apologize."

Wyatt sat up again. "What?"

"Can we not talk through the door? This feels stupid."

Wyatt flung the door open. Sebastian stood with his hands in his pockets. "What?"

"Look, I just want to say I'm sorry for the way I acted. I never should have gotten so angry with you. I should have never put my hands on you." Sebastian ran a hand through his hair and rubbed his face. "My dad is pissed at me because of my grades and he came down on me pretty hard. I'm sorry I took that shit out on you. I can't change the shit I've done but I can try to make it up to you."

Wyatt went to open his mouth, and sniffed the air. "Nikolai…"

"Yeah?" Nikolai poked his head around the door. "How do you always know, dude?"

"I thought you went back to Russia?" Wyatt hugged Nik tight.

"I did. Came back to kick Sebastian's ass," Nikolai winked. "Besides, isn't it your birthday?"

"*Was* my birthday," Wyatt grinned. "Did you get me a cake?"

"Nah, got you a male stripper, but you weren't here," Nikolai cracked up. "I can still strip for you, though," Nikolai waggled his eyebrows suggestively.

Wyatt eyed Nikolai's massive frame. "As good as that sounds…"

"Yeah, yeah, I know, I'm just a friend," Nikolai grimaced, taking Wyatt's hand. "You okay?"

Sebastian looked at the TV behind Wyatt. "Holy shit, man, is that at the pier?"

Wyatt turned to see the news on. A reporter was waving behind her at a building on fire. Wyatt turned the sound up.

"The building has been burning for over two hours now and firefighters are having trouble controlling the blaze; we've been told one firefighter is still in the building and may be injured."

Wyatt closed his eyes and opened the lines of communication. *"Preston..."* Wyatt waited hoping to hear anything from his mate. Nothing, not even a fleeting thought.

"I have to go, like, right the fuck now." Wyatt grabbed his cell phone and turned it on as he made his way down the stairs, out of the dorms, into the parking lot. The phone rang and he saw the Caller ID: 'Big Red.' Wyatt flipped the phone open. "Sean! Is it Preston?"

"Yeah, man," Sean turned around cupping the phone with his hand. "He needs you man; chief won't let us back in, it's too hot. Wyatt... Preston was hit in the head. I couldn't get the shit off of him and then a beam fell ..." Sean felt his throat closing up.

"I'm on my way!" Wyatt jumped in his truck and backed out of the parking area, tires squealing. He threw his hazards on and floored it. The drive had never seemed to take so long and Wyatt tried again and again to get through to Preston mentally. It was quiet and that scared him more than anything else. His mate was in trouble, trapped in a raging inferno, injured. Wyatt took side streets to the Alaskan Way Viaduct and then he saw it. The fire lit up the sky like daytime and Wyatt felt his heart pounding in his ears. He pulled off and parked two blocks over, running to the scene. Police were everywhere trying to push people back and Wyatt saw Sean.

"Sean!"

Sean pulled Wyatt alongside the building. "Come on!"

Wyatt ran, the heat searing his skin as he made his way closer to the mouth of the fire. "We lost him on the first floor, he got hit in the head and then another part of the ceiling came down in front of us. He's blocked in there, Wyatt, and we can't even get close enough to bust down the damn wall. We've been trying to douse the shit for hours but the bitch is hot."

Wyatt looked at Sean, then at the building on fire. He stripped his clothes off and handed them to Sean. "Hold these." Wyatt shifted and looked up to see Sean staring at him wide eyed. He turned and ran into the blaze, his nose working overtime trying to pinpoint Preston's location. He pushed the lines of communication open again, hoping to hear his mate. The fire licked at his tail as he ran. A long wooden beamed blocked his path and Wyatt stepped back and eyed it. He'd have to get some serious momentum. Head down, claws digging into the floor, Wyatt leapt with all his might and cleared the beam, singeing his tail on the way over.

He landed on the opposite side and finally saw Preston. His forehead was covered in blood and a beam lay across his torso, pinning him down. Wyatt shifted back and grabbed the beam throwing it like it was a feather. "Preston!" Wyatt got to his knees and assessed his mate. "I'm here, oh God, open your eyes, babe." Preston didn't move but

Wyatt knew he was alive; his pulse was slow, but Wyatt could hear it. He grabbed Preston in his arms and looked at the fire behind him. "Shit, shit, shit." Wyatt looked around and saw that the stairs to the floor above weren't on fire. He could do this.

Wyatt made his way up the stairs holding onto the railing with one hand. An explosion went off and Wyatt tightened his grip on Preston. The next floor was on fire as well but the window was somewhat clear. The glass had been shattered and Wyatt knocked the loose pieces off. Flames licked up his legs, searing his flesh as he grabbed hold of the window frame hauling up himself and Preston. He looked down and saw Sean below. "I got him!"

"Get out of there!" Sean shouted.

Wyatt steadied himself over the ledge as the intense fire moved in close enough to blister his back. He closed his eyes and, hanging onto to Preston tightly, he jumped. The ground rushed up to meet him and Wyatt landed hard on his feet, Preston's added weight making Wyatt's knees and ankles crack at the force of the landing. Wyatt put Preston down gently and looked him over. "He's probably got a concussion." Wyatt moved the bloody hair from Preston's face. A large gash was on the right side of his forehead.

"Wyatt, get your clothes on; let me get on the radio and get the EMTs over here." Sean handed Wyatt his clothing. "I thought you guys couldn't get hurt?"

"Of course we can! We can get knocked out just like anyone else. If he'd been conscious he could have made it out on his own. And if he'd been burned, he'd recover – but how would he explain it to everyone?" Wyatt yanked his pants on and got back to his mate. "I'm here," Wyatt kissed Preston's forehead. "I'm here and I'll never leave you again."

"Wyatt?" Preston opened his eyes and saw a blurry Wyatt crouched over him. "I heard you…"

"Listen, we don't have a lot of time." Wyatt kissed Preston's lips. "You have to tell them you got out on your own, okay? And for fuck's sake act injured."

Preston chuckled softly and wiped his head. "Shouldn't be too hard,"

"Are you okay?" Wyatt helped Preston to his feet.

"I am now," Preston caressed Wyatt's soot covered face. "Thank you, Wyatt."

"I love you." Wyatt pulled Preston into his arms and held him. It felt so damn good he never wanted to let go.

Sean coughed quietly and looked down the side of the building.

"Hey guys, this is sweet and all but we have to go. Wyatt, go all the way around and meet us by the ambulance okay?"

"Okay, see you in a few." Wyatt took one last look at Preston and ran.

"Well," Sean put his arm around Preston. "Let's hit it."

Chaos erupted as Sean walked out to the front of the building holding Preston up. Wyatt ran around the other side of the building and merged with the crowd before running into the group of firefighters. Sean nodded to Wyatt to get into the ambulance with Preston while he stayed behind to explain.

"We'll see you at the hospital, Wyatt," Sean winked. "It's good to see you, kiddo."

Wyatt smiled as the doors closed. He held Preston's hand and kissed the knuckles softly. The EMTs were setting Preston up with an IV and put an oxygen mask over his nose and mouth. Wyatt watched as they cleaned the blood off of Preston's forehead. One of them looked up and Wyatt gasped.

"Kellan?" Wyatt said.

"Yep, and Jude," Kellan motioned to his partner. "Scott's driving. Don't worry, Wyatt. He's going to be fine."

"Is he your boyfriend now?" Jude smiled.

Wyatt smiled and caressed Preston's face. "Yeah, he is." Wyatt watched the lights of Harborview Medical Center come into view and he leaned down to whisper into Preston's ear. "It's going to be okay, I love you."

Wyatt jumped out of the ambulance and followed as far as he could. He stood in front of the ER doors and watched as they took his mate away. Wyatt walked to the waiting room chairs and sat down in a daze. The reality hit and Wyatt broke down; the sobs wracked his body as he let out the pain of the last two weeks and the thoughts of the time he'd wasted being angry with Preston. Wyatt felt strong arms coming around him and looked up to see Sean's sad smile. Wyatt hugged Sean and cried. More and more firefighters arrived as the night wore on, most of them pacing the halls waiting for word. Wyatt was wearing a hole in the floor. He clenched and unclenched his hands waiting; he just wanted to see Preston. It seemed like days instead of hours and finally a doctor came out and cleared his throat.

"Mr. Dalton is going to be just fine. He has a concussion and some smoke inhalation but we are taking good care of him."

Wyatt ran to the doctor. "Can I see him please?"

"Are you Wyatt?"

"I am," Wyatt nodded.

"This way please," the doctor motioned through the doors.

Wyatt looked back at Preston's firefighter brothers and smiled at them. "I'll tell him you guys are all here." Wyatt followed the doctor down the hallway and they stopped in front of a door. Wyatt looked up at the doctor. "Thank you."

"I believe Preston's injuries would have been much worse if he was a normal human being," the doctor smiled. "But we both know that's not the case."

Wyatt's mouth dropped open. "Excuse me?"

The doctor put his hand out. "Doctor Alexander Romasko; it's a pleasure see you again, Wyatt."

"We've met?" Wyatt asked.

"You were much younger, but yes. My pack and I were in Denali, we merged with Wayne's pack as well as yours," Alexander smiled; Wyatt didn't believe him.

Wyatt stood there unable to speak until the doctor's eyes shifted to his lupine counterpart.

"Holy shit," he whispered.

"Take good care of him, Wyatt. You will be seeing me more often. We can't have mere humans poking around our anatomy now can we? I have sedated him, but he should be coming around soon. I can't have him up and running around right after an accident like that. Suspicious, don't you think?"

"Uh huh," Wyatt watched the doctor wink and make his way back toward the waiting room. Wyatt opened the door and saw Preston on the bed, an IV drip hung next to the bed and soft beeping could be heard. Wyatt took the chair next to the bed and took Preston's hand. "I'm here, Preston." Wyatt looked at Preston's beautiful face. He lifted the bandage from Preston's forehead; the cut had already healed. He smiled, taped it back down and looked at his mate's lips.

"I love you so much, Preston, I'm so sorry," Wyatt whispered. He kissed Preston's lips and closed his eyes, sending the message mentally. "I'm going to stay right here until you wake up." Wyatt crawled into the bed carefully and settled into Preston's warm body. He closed his eyes and hoped that the morning brought his mate back to him.

Chapter Nine

Preston's eyes opened to sunlight filtering across the bed. A hand was in his and he looked over to see Wyatt asleep, their fingers threaded together. Preston smiled and ran his free hand through Wyatt's soft hair. He could hear Wyatt's voice in his head even though he was asleep. Wyatt kept saying 'I love you' over and over. Wyatt moaned and moved his head as Preston ran his fingers through his hair and caressed his cheek.

"Hey, babe," Preston whispered.

Wyatt looked up. "You're awake."

"I am," Preston looked out the window. "How long have I been out?"

"Twelve hours. The doctor sedated you to keep you from running around," Wyatt grinned.

"That does sound like me." Preston caressed Wyatt's face. "I'm so sorry, Wyatt—"

"Don't," Wyatt put his arm over Preston's waist and snuggled into his neck. "I don't care anymore. The most important thing now is that we are together. I love you, Preston, and I'll never leave you again."

Preston kissed Wyatt's forehead. "Good, because I'm never letting you go."

"I wonder when you'll be discharged." Wyatt looked up at Preston and kissed his chin.

"Why, you got plans for me?" Preston smiled and pulled Wyatt closer to him.

"Oh yes," Wyatt pulled Preston to his lips. The kiss started slow and then a fire ignited in Wyatt as Preston's hands slid to his waist. His shirt was off and Preston was hovering over him before he knew what was happening. "Preston…" Wyatt breathed.

"We should take this to the apartment." Preston looked at Wyatt's sweat-covered face.

"Yes," Wyatt nodded. "We should do that."

"Good, because I want to show you how much I missed you," Preston nuzzled Wyatt's nose.

Wyatt sat up and glanced at the time. "I'll go find the doctor."

"Hurry," Preston smacked Wyatt's ass as he got out of the bed.

"Slut," Wyatt chuckled.

"Yup."

Preston got out of bed after Wyatt left and looked around the room. A duffle bag sat in the corner and he opened it finding his jeans and a T-shirt along with his sneakers. He slipped his clothing on and turned to see the door to his room open and his fellow firefighters smiling at him. Austin and Kurt grinned, along with Cole and Chaz. Sean walked over to him and hugged him.

"Dude, I thought for sure you'd be crispy," Sean kissed Preston's head.

"Aw come on guys," Kurt sighed. "You know I'm not used to that shit yet."

"Come here sexy," Austin grabbed Kurt.

"Ew! Get off!" Kurt laughed.

"Here?" Austin looked around and shrugged his shoulders. "Okay man, but if I get busted for jacking off…"

"Oh, for fuck's sake," Kurt sighed in frustration.

Sean chuckled. "We just saw Wyatt. He's filling out your release forms. So I take it everything's good?"

"Yeah," Preston smiled. "Everything's great." He eyed Kurt. "So how's Wesley?"

Kurt blushed. "Come on guys, you know we just hang out."

Sean eyed Kurt with a grin. "Dude, I'm not even gay and I can say that man is male model material."

"How is Olivia?" Preston nudged Sean.

"She's good, she sends her love," Sean winked.

They all looked at Kurt and waited.

"Oh, what?" Kurt threw his hands up in the air. "Look he took me out and I had fun, okay? He didn't kiss me or make a move on me and guys and chicks were checking him out all night!"

"Did he flirt with them?" Preston arched a brow.

"No, not once," Kurt blushed. "He totally ignored everyone but me."

"Did you get a woody?" Austin narrowed his eyes at Kurt.

Kurt shifted and covered his face with his hands. "No! Look, I'm not gay, all right?" Kurt looked at Preston.

"Why are you looking at me? Like I have gaydar and I'm supposed to know if you've come to the light side?" Preston sat down on the bed and put his shoes on.

Kurt looked at the guys in the room. "I'm not against what you are, let me make that clear. I'm just not into it. I came here thinking one way about gays and you enlightened me. I thank you for that. My parents raised me to think gays were sick," Kurt smiled at Preston. "I don't believe them anymore."

"Well good," Preston said. "Wesley's a good man and a damn good cop."

"Wait, he's a what?" Kurt said.

Preston smiled at the look of shock on Kurt's face. "Ah, so he didn't tell you what he does for a living."

"We talked about me the whole time," Kurt shook his head with a grin. "A cop, huh?"

"Yep, Tucker's a cop, too," Austin grinned.

"Ooooh, cops! I love cops," Chaz licked his lips.

"You love any guy with a cock," Cole rolled his eyes.

"As entertaining as this is," Preston looked at the group. "I need to get home and cuddle with my man."

"Aww," Sean hugged Preston. "I'm happy for you man."

Wyatt came back from the front desk and looked at the guys gathered around Preston.

"Did I miss something?" Wyatt eyed Austin and Kurt. "Why do you guys look like that?"

"Long story," Preston took Wyatt's hand. "Can I go now?"

"Yes, doctor signed off on your paperwork," Wyatt hugged Preston.

"You have a week off, Preston," Sean smiled. "Use the time wisely, and we'll see you back at the house." Sean hugged Wyatt. "Take good care of him," he whispered.

"Oh I will," Wyatt grinned.

"He's supposed to be getting rest, Quinton," Kurt laughed.

"He is?" Wyatt looked at Preston seductively. "You are?"

"Oh hell," Preston whispered. "Let's go."

~~

Preston shut the door to his apartment and turned to face Wyatt. There was one more thing they needed to do and Preston had no idea what would happen. He took a deep breath and walked into the kitchen, grabbing bottled water for himself and Wyatt. Wyatt was standing by the window looking out at the view of the university.

"You took this apartment to be close to me," Wyatt turned and looked at Preston. "Didn't you?"

"Yes, I did. I've wanted you for so long, Wyatt, but I knew I had to wait. You were too young to understand what being a mate actually meant. Shit, *I* was too young. Just understand this, I was never with anyone else, Wyatt, I have been true to you from the moment I figured out you were my mate."

"God, I'm sorry," Wyatt looked at the floor. "I was with Sebastian…"

"You didn't sleep with him, though. It's okay, Wyatt. I understand. There's something you need to know, though."

"What?" Wyatt walked over to Preston and stood in front of him.

"All this time I've been masking my scent so you wouldn't know who I was. I think it's time for me to let the wolf out, so to speak." Preston looked at Wyatt. "I have no idea what's going to happen when I do."

"Just do it." Wyatt took Preston's hand.

Preston closed his eyes and set his lupine side free. The temperature in the room went up immediately and he opened his eyes to see Wyatt looking at him. "Wyatt?"

"Oh shit," Wyatt whispered. Preston's scent assaulted his senses and his cock filled in seconds flat. His teeth elongated and his heart rate went through the roof. Preston smelled absolutely delicious. "Oh, Jesus, Preston."

"Oh, fuck."

Wyatt was on him in seconds. Preston hit the floor and Wyatt crawled up his body licking every inch of him. His clothes were literally torn off of him by Wyatt's claws and he struggled to breathe as Wyatt's mouth took his in a bruising kiss. Preston picked Wyatt up and threw him over his shoulder walking them to the bedroom. Wyatt was kissing and licking his back all while groping his ass. He threw Wyatt down on the bed and attacked him.

"Oh fuck, you smell so good," Wyatt tunneled his fingers into Preston's hair. "Make love to me."

Preston tore Wyatt's clothes off him and lunged at his weeping cock. He sucked in the engorged head and licked around the rim flicking at the sensitive nerve endings. Wyatt thrashed below him as he licked and nibbled Wyatt's erection, taking it in his hand and stroking it from root to tip. The salty taste of precum flowed over his taste buds and Preston groaned, sucking on the hardened rim. He fumbled for the nightstand drawer, grabbing the bottle of lube and coating his fingers with it. Wyatt's legs dropped open and Preston rubbed the heated crease, teasing Wyatt's opening.

He slid a finger in, twisting it, stretching Wyatt and looking for the spot that made him go crazy. His own cock was leaking with anticipation and he rubbed it on the comforter trying to get friction. The sight of Wyatt moaning on his bed was too much. He pulled his finger out, pushed Wyatt's legs up and dove for the pulsing hole his finger had just left. A hoarse cry reverberated in the room as Preston tongue fucked Wyatt's ass. He'd never done it before and now he couldn't stop, the noises Wyatt was making pushed him to go deeper, faster.

He licked, bit and chewed on Wyatt's ass until Wyatt's legs were shaking. Spreading Wyatt wider, he pushed his tongue in while his hand stroked Wyatt in time with it. He wanted to taste every last inch of his mate and when Wyatt cried out, Preston slid his cock in to the hilt. Wyatt went wild beneath him, bucking his hips and gripping his biceps tightly. Preston gripped Wyatt's hair in his hands and dove inside his mouth plunging into the warm cavern and sucking Wyatt's tongue. They ate at each other like a meal as Preston kept his thrusts short and shallow. It was wild and passionate and Preston wanted more; he gripped Wyatt's ass and picked him up, plunging his cock in deeper. Balls slapping skin, Preston fucked Wyatt with abandon. His muscles tensed and his balls drew taut. Wyatt exploded with a loud roar, shooting arcs of cum all over his chest and abs. Preston's orgasm took hold and he slammed into Wyatt; he almost screamed and he came so hard he nearly passed out from the intensity. Preston collapsed on top of Wyatt trying to catch his breath. He realized Wyatt was shivering underneath him and lifted his head, searching Wyatt's beautiful features.

"What's wrong, Wyatt? Did I hurt you?" Preston left light kisses all over Wyatt's face.

"I'm so happy," Wyatt cupped Preston's face in his hands. "I love you so much."

"I love you, too. I loved you from the moment I saw you, Wyatt Quinton. All the time we spent at the firehouse just enforced those feelings and then I fell *in* love with you. I knew the kind of man you would grow up to be." Preston kissed Wyatt softly and rubbed their noses together. "The day I shielded you in the forest changed my life. I knew I was going against Carson and I didn't care. My top priority was protecting my mate, even if he *was* only six," Preston chuckled softly.

"Almost seven," Wyatt pointed a finger at Preston.

Preston smiled as his fingertip did a slow exploration of Wyatt's face. "I went back to the pack and after Wayne took it over things got much better. I went back to school and when I turned eighteen I had your face put on me."

"The tattoo," Wyatt nodded.

"During the summer I'd take a trip down to see you but I always stayed far enough away so that you couldn't see me or smell me. I watched you grow up, Wyatt, and I never forgot you. Plus your dad sent me pictures of you over the years."

"He did?" Wyatt smiled.

Preston slid out of Wyatt's body slowly and kissed his face. He opened his closet and pulled out a wooden box. Sitting on the bed cross-legged he opened the box and took out pictures. "I love the eighth-grade rebellion one," Preston snickered.

Wyatt chuckled at the picture of himself with black eyeliner. "Yeah, well," Wyatt shrugged. "It didn't last long." Wyatt picked through all the pictures, amazed that Preston had kept them for so long. He even had a picture of Wyatt with Sebastian at a rival football game. Wyatt looked up at Preston. "This must have hurt you very much."

Preston sighed and lie back on the bed. "I think I was scared to death that you would fall in love before I could make myself known to you. When I saw Sebastian, I thought 'Well, that's it. I can't compete with those looks,'" Preston sighed.

Wyatt put the pictures down and crawled over to Preston, he hovered over him looking into his eyes. "No one is more beautiful than you." Wyatt ran his fingers through Preston's soft blond hair. "You have gorgeous eyes, soft, shiny hair and beautiful lips." Wyatt bent to kiss Preston's lips. "Not to mention a body that would stop traffic in San Francisco or any other place for that matter," Wyatt breathed across Preston's lips.

"Oh yeah, even Wyoming?" Preston flipped Wyatt onto his back and pinned him to the bed.

Wyatt pulled Preston down to his lips. "Especially Wyoming."

After what seemed like hours of kissing Preston finally succumbed to sleep, his mate by his side.

~~~~~

Preston opened one eye and looked at the clock. The green neon numbers told him it was almost noon. He stretched out lazily; he'd never slept in this late. A warm body next to him sighed softly and Preston wrapped Wyatt up in his arms, kissing his shoulder. He ran his hand down the soft, smooth skin of Wyatt's chest and tugged at a nipple. Wyatt chuckled and Preston pulled him over on his back. The seductive smile from Wyatt had Preston's engines revving.

"Jesus, you have no idea what you do to me," Preston cupped Wyatt's face.

Wyatt grinned. "Yes I do. I feel the same way. Do you know much I loved that last night? Just laying here in your arms and kissing? It made me feel closer to you."

"I have a confession," Preston kissed Wyatt's lips. "The first time I made love to you, I bit you."

"You did?" Wyatt sat up. "I don't remember that."

"Because you passed out right after your orgasm remember? I thought for sure you'd call me out on being a werewolf. Jesus, there were so many times I let that part of me escape, especially when Sebastian was around," Preston sighed and lay back. "I couldn't help myself."

Wyatt grinned and rolled over on top of Preston. "So I owe you a bite."

"Yes, I suppose you do." Preston ran his hands through Wyatt's silky hair. "I have a week off. We should go to the beach today. What do you say, huh? Then we can come back here and barbeque and make love."

"And I'll bite you," Wyatt waggled his eyebrows.

Preston flipped them over so he was on top again. He ground his hips into Wyatt's and smiled at Wyatt's erection on his hip. "Well, someone's already excited."

"Well, I *am* in bed with you." Wyatt closed his eyes as Preston's erection slid over his. "So, shower and then the beach?"

"Yes," Preston nuzzled Wyatt's neck and kissed his collar bone. "No work and all fun."

"Lead the way, my love," Wyatt put his hand out.

The shower took a lot longer than Wyatt had anticipated. Once under the hot spray they had started kissing again and Wyatt couldn't get enough of Preston's mouth. It blew Sebastian's kisses out of the damn hemisphere. Preston's kisses left him gasping and hanging onto the man with both hands as his body became boneless. They explored, caressed, licked and sucked until they both leaned against each other in an almost sex sedated haze. Wyatt finally turned the water off and exited the shower with Preston hanging onto him.

"My legs are numb," Wyatt laughed hanging onto the sink.

"Mine, too," Preston picked Wyatt up and deposited him on the edge of the counter. Grabbing the brush, he combed through Wyatt's short hair. "I loved it when it was long," Preston sighed running his fingers through it.

"I know, but I hate it long during football." Wyatt ran his fingers through Preston damp blond hair. "We are so different, Preston."

"Not really, our skin color is the only difference. Yours is like warm milk chocolate." Preston licked Wyatt's chest. "I can almost taste it."

"Does that make you white chocolate?" Wyatt grinned. "I'm kidding. Your skin is like a perfect vanilla latte." Wyatt ran his hands over Preston's soft skin. "I can't wait to get a tattoo of you."

Preston pulled Wyatt in his arms. "Oh, yeah? What will it look like?"

"A beautiful white wolf with brown eyes," Wyatt wrapped his arms around Preston's neck. "We better get going, sexy man."

"Hey, let's head down to Steilacoom. I haven't been down there in a while." Preston picked Wyatt up and walked them back into the bedroom.

"Okay, you drive." Wyatt grabbed some towels out of the linen closet.

"I'll get some water bottles." Preston walked into the kitchen. He stopped and looked at the apartment. Wyatt was his now, they had finally come together. "Hey, Wyatt?"

"Yeah?" Wyatt came into the kitchen and dropped the bag on the counter. "We have any finger foods?"

Preston pulled Wyatt into his chest. "We are together, right? Like exclusively?"

"Of course we are." Wyatt caressed Preston's face. "What is it?"

"Move in with me." Preston searched Wyatt's face.

"Anytime you want."

~~

The drive went by quickly and Wyatt took in the sights of Tacoma as they passed through it. He loved Washington, everything about it. June was heating up and Wyatt wiped his forehead. School would be starting up in late August and Wyatt wondered how he and Preston would be able to get around their schedules. They pulled into the parking area of Sunnyside Beach Park and Preston ran for the water. Even in the summer, the Sound wasn't very warm but it sure cooled you off when it was nearing one hundred outside. Wyatt laid the towels out and sank his toes into the warm sand.

Within fifteen minutes he was sweating and joining Preston in the cool water. Wyatt dove in and surfaced right next to Preston pulling his swim trunks down.

"Hey!" Preston grabbed Wyatt and crushed him to his chest.

"God, that's hot," Wyatt looked at Preston's bicep's flexing.

"Not so bad yourself." Preston ran his hands over Wyatt's broad back. "Who knew you'd look like this? You were so cute at ten, though."

"Hey! No fair, I didn't get to see you when you were ten." Wyatt wrapped his legs around Preston's hips linking his ankles together. "Kiss me."

Preston wrapped a hand in Wyatt's hair and pulled him to his lips. He hovered inches from Wyatt's mouth and smiled. "Service boy,"

"Oh, *hell* no." Wyatt crushed their lips together.

After making out in the water for a while, they sat back on the beach taking in the sun. Wyatt held Preston's hand and they talked about life. Wyatt wanted to know everything there was to know about Preston Dalton.

"Were you always a werewolf? Like me?"

Preston exhaled in sadness and raised his eyes to Wyatt's.

"I was at a party with Tucker and Wesley. At the time, my parents weren't really even paying attention to me, so the three of us would go out all the time. We found a party one night and kind of snuck in. I don't remember a lot, I had quite a bit to drink. But I remember waking up to find a guy on top of me. Next thing I knew, Wesley and Tucker and I were fighting wolves."

Preston shuddered. He pulled himself together and pressed on. "Wayne found us, sniffed us out so to speak, and took us to Carson. We stayed there and went back to school."

"I'm so sorry, Preston," Wyatt took Preston in his arms.

"My parents didn't even care," Preston whispered. "They told everyone I'd gone to live with my grandmother or something." Preston straightened up and forced a smile. "Doesn't matter. I had Wayne and the guys."

"And now you have me." Wyatt cupped Preston's face in his hands. "And you always will."

By sundown Wyatt could barely keep his eyes open and the drive back seemed to take forever. They both stumbled up the stairs to the apartment and barely made it into the shower to rinse off for bed. They'd go to the college in the morning to pack up Wyatt's things. Wyatt staggered out of the shower and collapsed on the bed.

"I'm so tired Preston," Wyatt moaned.

"I know, I think the sun drained me." Preston crawled on the bed and pulled Wyatt to his chest. "We can sleep in again."

Wyatt yawned. "Good, love you."

"Love you, too." Preston lay back and closed his eyes, the scent of Wyatt filling his senses.

~~~

"What do you think about me volunteering at the firehouse?" Wyatt shoved his clothing into his duffel bag.

Preston grabbed a box. "I think if it's what you want, then you should do it. You know I'm going to torture you, though."

"Oh, I know." Wyatt looked around the dorm room. "Well, I didn't have much to pack did I?"

The knock on the door spooked them both and they looked at each other.

"Sebastian," they both said.

Preston opened the door and looked at Sebastian in the hallway. "Yes?"

"Oh," Sebastian looked around Preston. "Um, hey, is Wyatt around?"

"That depends," Preston tapped his fingers on the door.

"I just wanted to make sure we were okay and shit. We are still on the same team and we have to get along. I'm glad you're okay, dude, I saw the fire." Sebastian backed into the hallway.

Preston relaxed his grip on the door. "Come in."

Sebastian looked around the room. "You moving out?"

"Yes," Wyatt picked up his books and put them in a box. "I'm moving in with my boyfriend."

Sebastian looked at the blond guy in the room. "Must be you?"

Preston nodded. "Sure is."

"Well," Sebastian put his hand out. "I know you'll treat him better than I did. He deserves that and so much more."

"I'll take good care of him." Preston shook Sebastian's hand.

"Well, I guess I'll see you in August for football practice?" Sebastian looked at Wyatt. "I am sorry, Wyatt, you didn't deserve the way I treated you." Sebastian ran a hand through his hair. "I wish you all the best. I'm going to be spending some time with George; he invited me out to his house," Sebastian said.

Wyatt grinned. "He's a good man; he's always been nice to me. He treats you like his own kid."

"He always has, he's been like a father to me. Which I'm sure irritates my dad to no end; the butler-servant man treats me better than he does," Sebastian said.

Wyatt took Sebastian's hand. "I'll have your back on the field, Bastian, and off," Wyatt smiled.

"You're a good friend," Sebastian wiped his eyes. "I gotta go."

Preston watched Sebastian leave the room. "That was odd."

"Yeah, it was." Wyatt looked at Preston and frowned. "I know he's having issues with his dad, but something else is freaking him out."

"Maybe you can talk to him about it?"

"Yeah, maybe," Wyatt looked around the room. "Well this is it." Wyatt motioned to the three boxes and duffel bag. "I don't have much."

"It will all fit and I want you to go shopping with me and pick up stuff you like okay? Our apartment will have things you like in it." Preston hugged Wyatt. "I can't believe this is real. I'm actually holding you in my arms and you're moving in with me."

Wyatt smiled. "It's just the beginning, Preston."

~~

By the time they made it back to the apartment they were half naked just walking up the stairs to their unit. As soon as the door shut Wyatt was all over him. This time, Preston felt his feet leaving the floor as Wyatt carried him down the hall to their bedroom. He hit the bed with a bounce, and Wyatt jumped on top of him. Preston let out a breath and looked at Wyatt's lust-filled eyes.

"How do you want me?"

"On your back," Wyatt growled. "I want to see your face. Later on, when we get all crazy and shit, I'll get us a sex swing and a stripper pole."

"Wait, which one of us is stripping?" Preston arched a brow.

"You are," Wyatt pointed at Preston.

"Oh, hell, no."

Wyatt laughed.

Preston moaned in ecstasy as Wyatt made love to him. He slid in like silk and the ride was one he'd never forget. Wyatt kept his thrusts slow and controlled, filling him to the hilt and sliding back out rubbing his cockhead along every ridge in his ass. His prostate was massaged on every in-stroke and Preston gripped the sheets with a scream on his lips. His orgasm rocked him to the core and when Wyatt's canines sunk into him, Preston came again with a howling moan. The power rode up his spine and exploded out his fingertips. The connection was so strong Preston felt his heart ramming in his ribs. He wrapped his arms around Wyatt and kissed his neck.

"God, I fucking love you so damn much," Preston sighed.

"I love you too, Preston." Wyatt ran his lips up the soft flesh he'd just bitten. "We are connected for life, babe."

"I wouldn't have it any other way."

Wyatt smiled looking into Preston's eyes. "We are all connected now. You, Taylor and Jagger, we're all a family now. You're not alone anymore, Preston." Wyatt caressed Preston's face.

"I'm going to marry you." Preston cupped Wyatt's face in his hands.

"You'd better," Wyatt smiled.

Chapter Ten

July Fourth found the men of the firehouse on Austin's pontoon boat anchored off of Gas Works Park. Wyatt's family joined them along with Nicholas, Tucker, Wesley and Olivia. Wyatt made sure everyone's drink was topped off. He was the designated boat driver for the evening and was pounding the Dr Peppers down. Now that Wyatt knew the whole story, he knew that Tucker and Wesley were the other kids Preston had run away with. They were a close-knit group, to say the least. Austin seemed a little more open towards Tucker and Kurt was coming around a little day by day to Wesley. They definitely had their work cut out for them with two straight mates. But Wyatt could see that Austin truly liked Tucker, and if the feelings were already there it may not be such a far jump for Austin. Tucker and Wesley were going back to Anchorage the following day and Wyatt hoped that they'd made a big enough impression for Austin and Kurt to at least be thinking about them when they left.

Sean was dating Olivia exclusively and took over the job of keeping her safe from horny underclassman. He promised to visit her at school when it resumed, making his presence known. Wyatt had gotten over his anger at everyone knowing about his mate and keeping him in the dark. It didn't matter anymore, he loved Preston. The Sound was filled with shouts and laughter as more boats pulled up and anchored nearby. The fireworks show at Gas Works Park was a must-see on July Fourth. They came out early in the day and grabbed a prized area. Taylor and Jagger were fishing off the back of the boat and Grayson grabbed a beer for his husband, lowering it in front of his face.

"You there, babe?" Grayson kissed Taylor's head.

"Oh, yes. Jagger keeps catching dogfish sharks," Taylor elbowed his brother.

"Yeah? Well you keep catching those freaky-eyed fish." Jagger took a swig of his beer.

"Freaky eyes?" Grayson looked at his husband. "You mean flounder?"

"Yeah, they freak me out," Jagger chuckled. "I refuse to eat them."

Xander came up on the conversation and chuckled.

"He won't, I can't even secretly cook flounder. I swear he just looks at it and knows." Xander sat down by his husband and kissed his cheek. "Love you, babe."

Jagger set up his pole and dragged Xander into his lap. "And I love you." Jagger ran his hand through his husband's jet black hair. "I swear those eyes got me the minute you looked at me."

"What is it with those eyes?" Taylor pulled Grayson down.

Troy and Sawyer joined in, sitting down with the group.

"I know, the minute I laid eyes on Sawyer I knew he was it." Troy wrapped his arms around Sawyer.

"My mom's eyes," Sawyer sighed. "We were all blessed with the emeralds."

"And we are all gay," Grayson snickered. "Poor Dad."

"Well, we plan on getting a surrogate," Troy kissed Sawyer's neck. "We are going to have another rambunctious baby Wyatt running around."

A loud groan came from the group. Wyatt looked at his brothers.

"I was *not* that bad!" Wyatt smacked Xander's head.

"Ow! Abuse! Dad!" Xander laughed and moved out of the way of another smack.

John Quinton looked at his sons and smiled.

"I love all of you. I'm proud to be your father." John put his arms out. "Give your old man a hug."

"I got him first!" Wyatt ran.

~~

Kurt watched as more boats pulled up, anchoring nearby. Seattle was different than Wyoming, by a long shot. He and Austin were contemplating moving in together to save money. Austin was cool; they had almost the exact background. A beer appeared in front of him and he turned to see Wesley grinning.

"Thanks," Kurt said.

"Welcome."

"So, Wyatt says you and Tucker are going back to Alaska?"

Wesley nodded, sipping his beer. "Back to work, I can come out for Christmas, you know if you want?"

Kurt looked into Wesley's eyes, they were a beautiful combination of cognac and amber; his hair was a shade Kurt had never seen before, a rich mahogany. "I... look; I don't know how to say this without hurting your feelings. I'm not gay and I don't want you to think there's something here."

Wesley backed away a little; his heart felt like someone had reached inside him and squeezed it. "Oh, okay. I just thought, you know, maybe as friends or something."

Kurt opened his mouth, only to be interrupted by Austin joining them with Tucker.

"What's up, punk?" Austin hip-bumped Kurt.

"I was just telling Kurt that Tucker and I are planning on coming back for Christmas," Wesley said.

"Yeah?" Austin looked at Tucker.

"Well, just for a week maybe," Tucker quickly said.

"That could be cool," Austin nodded.

"Really?" Tucker asked.

"Well, yeah, why not? I'm not going home for Christmas; I can't stand being in the same room with my parents," Austin laughed. "How about you, Kurt?"

Kurt looked from Austin to Wesley. "I'm not sure yet." Kurt took Austin aside, looking over his shoulder at Wesley and Tucker. "You know he's gay right? If you agree to go out with him again, he's going to expect things from you."

Austin grinned. "I told him I'm not gay, sheesh. What is wrong with you?"

"Nothing," Kurt said.

"Look, Tucker's a great guy, I have fun with him. There's nothing wrong with having fun with another man."

~~

Wesley looked over at Tucker; both of them could hear the conversation like it was right in front of them.

"Face it, Tucker. They aren't gay; it's never going to happen," Wesley said sadly.

Tucker closed his eyes. "It's not fair."

"Life isn't fair. Let's just face it, the fates screwed us over."

Tucker walked to the bow of the boat and looked over the water. He had a mate, a mate who wanted nothing to do with him. "Fuck."

As the sun set over the Sound, the guys made their seating arrangements. Wyatt sat between Preston's legs and relaxed into his chest. Their fingers threaded together as Preston wrapped him up in his arms.

"You happy?" Preston nuzzled Wyatt's ear.

"Never been happier," Wyatt looked up at his mate and warm lips covered his.

The first burst of color hit the sky above and Wyatt watched in awe. Music played in sync with the fireworks and more went off, bigger blasts with more color and flair. Wyatt was wrapped in the arms of his mate, they were a family. Preston had had a horrible childhood from the moment he admitted the truth to his parents. Alone in the world until Jagger, Taylor, Wesley and Tucker entered his life, he was then presented with a mate six years his junior. Wyatt was going to make sure Preston never wanted for anything. He squeezed Preston's fingers and leaned against the strong, warm chest behind him. Preston's nose was nuzzling his hair and Wyatt tipped his face up.

"I'm sorry I got mad at you, Preston. I really do understand why you kept yourself hidden. It must have been hard on you to stay away."

Preston smiled. "Oh God, when you turned fourteen," Preston shook his head and chuckled. "You were already so damn beautiful. I knew if I'd let you know who I was, I wouldn't be able to keep my hands to myself."

"I was really horny, too," Wyatt snickered.

"Yeah, I know," Preston sighed loudly. "I used to stay upwind of you so you couldn't smell me, but boy could I smell you." Preston let out a low whistle. "Hot damn, baby."

Wyatt laughed, leaning back into Preston again. He wiggled, feeling something sharp on his spine. "What is that?"

Preston removed the box from his front pocket. "Your birthday gift. I was going to give it to you that night, but…"

Wyatt opened the box. A platinum band sat on a bed of cotton. Wyatt raised his eyes to Preston's. "I love you, Preston Dalton," Wyatt whispered.

"I love you too, Wyatt, always."

~~Epilogue~~

Wyatt shielded his eyes from the Arizona sun. Even though it was December, the air was slightly warm. Derek and James Jacobs were taking their marriage vows once again, this time in front of family and friends in the Chiricahua Mountains. He had to admit, it was beautiful - rocks seemed to hang suspended in midair.

The sun was slowly setting and the sky was beautiful; shades of orange and lavender spread across the mountain peaks. Derek and James' official wedding had been in Canada not too long after Vince Markov had married Keegan Ripley. The entire group had made the time to attend this ceremony in Arizona. It had started with the Skull Blasters - Mateo, Josh, Sam and Troy, and now the family had extended to include everyone. Christmases were spent flying between Denali, Washington and Arizona as the packs, and the humans, became family.

Wyatt felt Preston's hand in his; they were engaged and would be getting married on the beach on Queets land. Things had come together quite nicely. The wolf who had covered him protectively when he was seven had become his fiancé. He was back in school, playing football and mending his relationship with his ex-boyfriend, Sebastian.

Nadine stood with Joe, watching the ceremony with tears in her eyes. Wyatt's extended family adored Preston and was already hounding them for kids. His brothers stood with their husbands, all of them still so happy and in love. Wyatt's eyes found Tucker and Wesley watching the ceremony; they had both found their mates only to discover that they were straight. Wyatt could tell that Austin had feelings for Tucker; he just couldn't put a name to them yet. Kurt had kept to himself a lot after Wesley had gone back to Anchorage, and Wyatt would catch him occasionally looking at the pictures from the firehouse barbeque. Meanwhile, Tucker and Wesley waited and hoped for a miracle.

A slight squeeze from Preston's hand alerted him to the end of the ceremony. Wyatt clapped as James and Derek shared a kiss. The wedding party moved to a bed and breakfast down the road for the reception. Ever the proper host, Riley ushered everyone into the main dining room and champagne was poured. Josh, Mateo, Sam and Troy had served as Derek's best men, and Riley had stood with James. The men all settled in and Riley raised his glass to Derek and James.

"We were all fortunate enough to watch the love story between Derek and James come to fruition. I'm sure I speak for all of us when I say it's about time!"

There was a collective chuckle from the guests.

"So, let's raise our glasses and give a toast to two men who went through hell and came out on the other side more in love than ever!"

"Hell, yeah!" Josh shouted, downing his champagne.

Wyatt's eyes roamed the room as he sat chatting about work with Preston, Tucker, Wesley and Nicholas. Keegan's FBI partner, Special Agent Devin Lyons, was up getting food and Wyatt's eyes widened as he saw an accident ready to happen. He sprang from the table but arrived too late as Lyons turned and ran right into Vince's ex-husband and Devin's nemesis: Andrei Panchenko. Red fruit punch splattered between the two of them and Devin's cake landed on Andrei's chest.

"Son of a bitch!" Devin growled. "Watch where you're going!"

"*You* ran into *me*!" Andrei shoved Devin backwards.

Wyatt tried desperately to stop the fight before it became a full-out brawl. It didn't work. Fists were flying as Devin and Andrei took their scuffle to the floor. Vince jumped in, along with Keegan, and Wyatt was pulling Devin off of Andrei.

"I'm going to kill you!" Andrei roared.

Devin laughed. "Good luck with that!"

"You were supposed to get along!" Keegan shouted. "It's Derek's and James' special day, goddammit!"

Devin caught Andrei's eyes and noticed him slowly licking Devin's blood off of his knuckles.

Devin smirked. "Is that supposed to scare me? Cause I gotta tell ya – I'm a little turned on right now."

Keegan sighed in frustration and glared at Devin, who looked down at the floor and clasped his hands together like a penitent toddler. "I'm sorry."

James stepped in between Andrei and Devin. "You two are going to have to try and get along somehow; you're on the same team now."

"I'll never trust that murdering bastard," Devin snarled.

Andrei chuckled. "Me? Look who's talking, Agent Lyons. I have seen your kill record - you and Vince could be in competition. In fact, you are actually worse than he is. At least Vince can *feel.*"

"Yeah? No thanks to you – he had to meet another man to accomplish that!"

"Both of you, time out, right now," Nikolai grabbed Andrei, leading his father away.

Derek eyed Devin. "Devin?"

"I'm sorry. I know I should have just walked away."

"No harm, no foul. No alcohol was spilled in the fight," Josh grinned, leading Devin away from the group and breaking the tension.

Wyatt smiled at James and Derek. "Never a dull moment, huh?"

"When did you get so grown up?" James hugged Wyatt. "Thanks for coming."

"Preston and I wouldn't have missed it. You two are coming to our wedding, right?"

Derek took Wyatt by the shoulders. "We wouldn't dare miss you marrying your mate. It's a love story years in the making."

"Yes," Preston said. "Eleven *very long* years."

"And you love each other; you always will." James mussed Wyatt's short hair.

"Trust me, it didn't start out that way," Wyatt smiled at Preston. "I hated him in the beginning." Wyatt furrowed his brows. "You know, that gives me an idea."

"Uh oh," Preston laughed.

"No, seriously. Dad used to put me and my brothers in a room when we were fighting and let us have it out. Maybe you could do the same with Devin and Andrei?"

James snorted. "They would kill each other."

"Maybe Devin needs anger management?" Preston offered.

"No psychiatrist will even be in the same room with Devin Lyons," Derek arched a brow. "They are scared shitless of him."

Wyatt looked over at Josh talking with Devin. "He doesn't seem that scary."

"The Bureau wanted him out and locked away because he's so volatile and completely unpredictable. He's a loose cannon. The only reason he walks around free is because of James; he seems to be the only one Devin really listens to. He's just as vicious as Vince and is the number one assassin for the FBI," Derek explained.

Wyatt looked Devin Lyons over. The man was maybe five foot ten with dirty blonde hair, pale grey eyes and a muscular physique. He didn't look *that* scary.

"Don't let his looks fool you," James cautioned, following Wyatt's line of sight. "He's as deadly as they come - and you never see him coming."

Wyatt shivered, snuggling into Preston. "I'll take your word for it."

By the time Wyatt hit the bed at the bed and breakfast, it was three in the morning. He threw an arm over Preston, pulling him closer. They were already talking about having kids, but Wyatt wanted to wait until he graduated from college. Just the thought of having a little Preston running around made him smile.

"I want a little Wyatt, too." Preston kissed Wyatt's forehead, yawning.

"We agreed we'd have your child first." Wyatt tweaked Preston's nipple.

"Ow," Preston chuckled. "Yes we did and I can't wait to start a family with you."

"You think we'll be good parents? With both of us being firefighters?"

"I think we'll be excellent parents."

Wyatt yawned, burying his face in Preston's neck. "I think so, too. You deserve to have everything you've ever wanted, Preston. You have love now; my dad loves you as his own and my brothers treat you like another brother."

"Yes they do; could you ask them to lay off the pranks?" Preston said, chuckling.

"Now why would I do that?" Wyatt chuckled.

Preston rolled over on top of Wyatt, pinning him beneath him. "I think I want to make love until morning."

"Oh, the horror."

"I love you, Wyatt."

"Me, too. Now, get to showing me that love."

~The End~

Sneak Peek: Reflash

"Oh my God! What the hell? How is this stupid thing still alive?" Wesley shook his phone. "It got hit in the head with a rock! Stupid pig! Now it's laughing at me, just great." Wesley banged his head on the steering wheel.

Tucker sipped his coffee and grinned at his partner from the passenger seat of the squad car. They had been in Seattle for almost a month. The change from Anchorage PD to Seattle's wasn't difficult; in fact, it was easier. Their friend Nicholas had talked to his boss and Tucker and Wesley were partnered. Once they'd figured out their mates were in Washington, it had become a priority to move closer. Austin Jacobson was a fireman, and Tucker's mate. He was also straight, as was Wesley's mate, Kurt Maguire.

Tucker snickered. "You do realize how that sounds, right?"

Wesley looked over at Tucker. "Huh?"

"Stupid pig?" Tucker raised an eyebrow.

"It's *Angry Birds*!" Wesley shoved his phone in Tucker's face. "I swear I'm angrier than the birds are!"

"Stop playing that, it's almost as bad as when you were addicted to *Tetris*. That stupid song was in my head for *months*!" Tucker caught sight of a car speeding up the road behind them. "Flash him."

Wesley hit the lights as the car flew by them, the brake lights flashed and the car slowed down. Wesley chuckled, looking over at Tucker. "Wonder what they were in a hurry for?"

Tucker shrugged. "Hot date?"

"Speeding home to jack off?" Wesley put his phone down and looked over at Tucker. They'd been best friends from the day they met. "When should we call them? How are we going to do this? Kurt's been out with me twice maybe and I don't know what to do. I want him so much."

Tucker ran his hands over his face. "You think I don't want to call Austin? I'm not sure what to do anymore. Right now we wait and see if the fates throw us together somehow. We've gone out with them, played it cool and kept our hands to ourselves. We can't do much more than that, Wes. They are straight for fuck's sake."

Wesley rolled his eyes. "You don't have to keep reminding me my mate is straight, and almost homophobic. At least Austin's a little better with you."

Tucker sat back and brought forth a vision of Austin Jacobson. Six feet of pure muscle, dark hair and light blue eyes. Tucker sighed and pinched his cock. "I can't even think about him without getting hard."

"Kurt's just…" Wesley sat back, looking at the roof of the squad car. "I mean he's not mean or anything, he just is kinda standoffish."

Tucker was about to open his mouth, when he spotted a car weaving on the road. He smacked Wesley in the shoulder and grinned. "Bets?"

"Over the limit for sure." Wesley watched the car pass them, oblivious to the squad car parked right off the side of the road.

"Let's do it." Tucker strapped in and Wesley started the car. The lights were on and the siren blared. The car was still weaving in and out of both lanes and Wesley got right up on its back end. The driver finally pulled over to the side and Tucker got out. He walked to the driver's side and shined his flashlight in the car. The driver still had the window rolled up and Tucker knocked on it with the flashlight, making the motion with his hand to roll the window down. The window lowered slowly and Tucker got a good look at the occupant. Cute kid, maybe nineteen or twenty, was looking at him with red, glazed eyes. He smelled like a whiskey mill.

"License and registration, please."

Tucker had to hold in a laugh as the kid almost fell off the seat onto the floorboard opening the glove compartment. He sat up shakily and handed the information over. Tucker looked at the driver's license with a frown. Will Cooper was twenty one; had just turned twenty one, as a matter of fact, at midnight.

"Will, could you do me a favor and step out of the vehicle, please?" Tucker stepped away from the side of the car. He motioned to Wesley to come over. Will, or William, stepped out of the car and almost fell over. Tucker heard Wesley snickering on his way over. "You wouldn't have been drinking tonight, Will, now would you?" Tucker asked. Will's glazed eyes looked at Tucker.

"God, you're smokin' hot," William said.

Standing with his arms crossed, Wesley chuckled looking over the younger man. Tucker handed him the kid's ID.

"Well, happy birthday, Will. Say, why don't you do us a favor and stand over here on the yellow line?"

"Wow," William licked his lips, looking at Wesley. "This is like a total fantasy of mine."

"Is that right?" Tucker arched a brow.

"Having two cops do me on a squad car," William stumbled to the yellow line.

Wesley looked over at Tucker and tilted his head. He smiled when Tucker shook his head no. Wesley sighed and threw his hands up in the air. "Okay, William. Stand on one foot." Wesley covered his mouth as William stood on the line, one foot up. "Now, put both your arms out to your sides." Wesley waited for William to comply, then gave him more instruction. "Now, take your finger and put it on your nose."

"Jump up and down at the same time," Tucker added. William promptly fell over and moaned. Tucker walked over to him and smiled. "Sorry bud, you get to spend the night in jail."

"Fuck," Will slurred. "Can I at least get my fantasy? Maybe avoid a cell?"

"Will, are you a virgin?" Tucker asked.

"Tucker!" Wesley whispered.

"What? He's not going to remember this anyway." Tucker looked at Will, trying to stand up on the yellow line again. "Will?"

"Yeah?"

"Virgin?"

"Pfft…no."

"Not much of a bribe then, huh?" Tucker chuckled.

"Jesus, Tucker! I'll call the tow," Wesley laughed, walking back to the squad car.

Tucker helped William up, walking him toward the car. "What were you thinking? Drinking and driving?"

William sagged in Tucker's grip.

"Today I told my now not-very-happy parents I was gay and my boyfriend broke up with me tonight." William looked up at the officer currently holding him up. "Aren't you going to cuff me? Read me my Melinda rights?"

"It's Miranda, and I don't think you're running off anywhere; I doubt you'll remember your rights but I'll read them to you." Tucker helped William into the car after he'd read him his rights. He leaned over and pulled William's startled face up. "Don't let it get you down; I'm sure there's another guy out there perfect for you and your parents will eventually get over it."

"I need coffee," William whined.

"Well, I'm going to give you a breathalyzer before I allow you to drink coffee," Tucker smiled.

"I'm drunk, I admit it," William sighed, and promptly passed out on the back seat.

"Well, that was fun." Wesley looked at the time. "Only four more hours to go!"

"Why did we take this shift again?" Tucker pulled the seatbelt over his lap, clicking it into place.

"We love the night life?" Wesley chuckled, and pulled onto the road.

"I love the night life, I like to boogieee!" Tucker sang, looking out the window. After being in Seattle for over a month, he missed seeing Austin. They hadn't called or spoken to each other since the Fourth of July; it'd been almost a year. Tucker closed his eyes; he wanted his mate. The sad part was, he didn't think his mate would ever want him.

~~

"Fuck! It's hot as hell!" Austin swore his skin was melting. The fire was raging in the small apartment complex they'd been called to and three hours later, were still trying to put it out. Kurt was in front of him, leading them out. They'd gotten everyone out of the building, including two pet rats. Austin had sent them out with Preston; he wasn't a huge fan of rodents. "Where the fuck is probie?"

Kurt kicked the door open and walked out into a rain of water and smoke. "He's out! I made him leave."

"Jesus Christ!" Austin tore his mask off. "What the hell!" Austin walked over to the rig. He grabbed a bottle of water and poured it down his face. He took a deep breath of semi-clean air and coughed. Kurt smacked him on the back and Austin glanced at him sideways. Kurt leaned up against the rig, taking in deep breaths. "What happened in there?" Austin asked.

"He froze, that's what happened." Kurt drank a half bottle of water before resuming. "The sight of that old lady freaked him out. He thought she was dead."

"She's burned badly," Austin nodded. "That's a sight even I'm not used to yet, but he can't freeze up like that!" Austin stripped out of his turnouts, and pulled his sweat soaked T-shirt over his head. The new guy, or probie, as he was called, was almost twenty three-and still green around the gills when it came to death. As a firefighter, it was something you had to see now and then and Austin didn't think he'd ever get used to it. It didn't mean he couldn't do his job, though. Probie, Dean Anderson was his real name, had been at the house for six months and it had been Austin's profound pleasure to inflict on him what he himself had endured during his probie stage.

"I'm so ready to go home," Austin said.

"Three off, what do you want to do?" Kurt asked.

"Sleep," Austin chuckled, dragging his fingers through his dirty hair.

"Yeah? Me, too, except we have to clean this week." Kurt removed his own turnouts and wiped the sweat from his brow with his forearm. "Your turn to clean the toilet."

"Whatever." Austin leaned against the truck, closing his eyes. He and Kurt had moved in together not long after Kurt had come to the firehouse. They were both neat freaks and the situation had worked out well for both of them. They took turns driving to work and who bought the groceries. They got along well, too. Both from small towns in anti-gayish communities, they had a lot in common. Austin brought up a vision of Tucker at the thought of gays; it'd been happening a lot lately. He hadn't heard from him in months. After the Fourth of July on the Sound, Tucker and Wesley had gone back to work in Anchorage. Austin smiled to himself; Tucker had been every bit the gentleman whenever they'd gone somewhere together. He never tried to touch him, always stayed a few feet away when they walked. Tucker had the most beautiful eyes - hazel, but gold seemed to flare out in the iris, making them mesmerizing.

"Where'd you go?" Kurt asked, looking over at Austin's smile.

"Um, nowhere," Austin straightened up.

Kurt narrowed his eyes. "The bullshit flag just went up. Spill it, Jacobson. I know what you've been thinking about lately."

Austin swallowed hard. "You do?"

"Yes, I do. You're trying to think of how many ways you can tell Nina 'no' before she actually believes you," Kurt laughed.

Austin relaxed and grinned. "She's an animal! We went out one time and her hands were down my pants within the first two seconds. I swear she sucked the skin right off my prick!"

"Oh, you poor thing!" Kurt rolled his eyes.

Kurt threw his gear in the rig and turned to look at his roommate. He actually liked Austin a lot; they had so much in common it was ridiculous. They were close in age as well, Austin was twenty-four and he was twenty-six. They ate the same food, drank the same beer and watched the same shows. Austin was the roommate heaven sent. He'd met Austin's mother one time when she came to visit. Austin's mother was a lot like his own mother - the Sunday churchgoing, Bible thumping, gays-are-an-abomination kind. Kurt had never been so happy to see that woman pack up and leave. No wonder Austin left home as fast as he could; it was the same reason he himself had.

Kurt looked at himself in the rig's shiny bumper. He was pretty good-looking he supposed. He wasn't as hot as Wesley Foster, though. Kurt cringed. And there he went again. He'd found

186

himself thinking more and more about Wesley over the last few months - the way he smiled, the waves in his beautiful mahogany-colored hair and the eyes... Kurt almost sighed; Wesley had the most beautiful eyes. A cognac-colored brown with hints of amber flecks. Just beautiful. Kurt could see Wesley's face as if he were standing right next to him. Wesley was taller than him as well, at least six foot two and muscles that seemed to come out from all directions. Kurt looked at himself again; pale blue eyes looked back from a face that looked tired and weary. This was the third suspicious-looking fire in three months' time and they'd been working extra shifts, trying to keep up with the ones that popped up in between. Kurt caught the reflection of Chief Webber standing behind him and straightened up.

"Maguire."

"Yes, sir?" Kurt said.

"You and Jacobson pack it in; we're heading back to the house. I don't want to see you two, at all, for three days."

"Sir?"

"You look like shit."

Kurt managed a half-smile. "Thanks, Chief."

By the time they got back to the firehouse, it was almost six in the morning. Kurt took a quick shower and waited for Austin to get his shit before they both headed out to the parking lot. Slipping into Austin's gold Excursion, Kurt looked over at his roommate. "Club this weekend?"

"One night only. I want to go camping."
Austin started the truck.

"Again with the camping? I fish, I don't
camp," Kurt said.

"Camping and fishing then; stop being a big
baby," Austin chuckled, pulling out of the parking
lot.

"I am not a big baby," Kurt crossed his arms
and pursed his lips.

"Friday night club with the guys, then
camping. No excuses this time!" Austin playfully
punched Kurt in the shoulder.

"Is it gay or straight week?" Kurt chuckled.

Austin tilted his head in thought. "I forgot,
but who cares?"

"Not me, I've been there so many times, the
gay guys know I'm straight and they ward off the
ones who don't."

"At least you got some tips on how to dress
better," Austin laughed.

Kurt looked down at his jeans. He had to
admit, when Cole and Chaz had taken him
shopping, he had looked damn good. He'd gotten
some clothing he'd never thought he'd wear, but
looking at himself in the mirror, he realized he
liked the look. And it had actually gotten him a ton
of dates. The firefighter status got him laid all the
time; the clothes were an added bonus.

"True," Kurt nodded. "I see Chaz got you
into Hollister as well."

"He did. Damn that store is dark as hell!" Austin said.

"They don't want you to be able to see the price tags," Kurt laughed. "Cole got me all Bananad."

"Huh?" Austin glanced over at Kurt.

"Dolce and Bananad."

Austin almost threw up he was laughing so hard. As it was, he pulled over until he could regain his breath. "That's Dolce and Gabbana."

"Whatever!" Kurt sighed, exasperated. "I never wear that stuff, but damn if my ass isn't juicy in those jeans."

Austin held his gut as the laughter kept pouring from him. "Stop! I have to get us home."

"You wanna wear my bananas Friday?" Kurt cracked up.

"Shup," Austin laughed.

Pulling up to their condo, Kurt spotted a very familiar looking Chevy truck. He let out a loud, exasperated sigh. "Oh, shit."

"What's up?" Austin pulled into their parking space.

"My dad is here." Kurt exited the vehicle. The door on the Chevy passenger side opened and Kurt smiled. His younger brother, Kory, got out smiling wide.

"Nugget!" Kurt opened his arms.

"Asshole!" Kory ran into Kurt's arms, hugging him tightly.

189

Kurt hugged his brother. "God, you got huge!" Kurt looked up, seeing his father with his hands on his hips, a frown already in place. Kenneth Maguire was a pastor and ruled with an iron fist.

"Dad."

"What did I say about cursing, Kory?" Kenneth pursed his lips.

"Sorry," Kory said.

"What brings you here, Dad?" Kurt put his hand out, shaking his father's. There was no hugging in the Maguire house. Kurt hugged his brother anyway. He was twenty-six and no longer lived under the same roof. Screw it; he'd do whatever the fuck he wanted. "This is my roommate, Austin Jacobson."

"Pleasure to meet you, sir." Austin put his hand out.

"Roommate?" Kenneth's brow rose.

"Yes, Dad. We work together at the firehouse, made sense to get a place together. Austin's from Montana." As sad as it was, his father seemed to relax at that statement, as if no one in Montana was gay.

"Good to meet you, Austin." Kenneth turned his attention back to his sons. "I'm running the youth Christian camp again. Kory decided he didn't want to go be a counselor, he'd rather visit his big brother."

"Well he's more than welcome to stay," Austin smiled at Kurt's younger brother. "How old are you?"

"Just turned nineteen," Kory beamed.

"Yes and he's reckless and irresponsible already. Doesn't want to work in the church anymore." Kenneth narrowed his eyes at Kory.

"I'm nineteen, Dad. I want to go to college; I want to be a fireman like my brother," Kory set his jaw tight. "Like my grandfather."

"And what did that get him? A life cut short fighting fires," Kenneth's voice rose. "Died, trying to save an old woman."

"At least he died doing what he loved," Kurt crossed his arms over his chest. "I'll watch Kory, Dad. Have fun at camp."

"Don't let him go out on his own, I've heard all about Seattle." Kenneth stalked back to his truck.

Kurt put his arm around Kory, watching his father pull out of the parking lot without so much as a wave goodbye. It didn't surprise him one bit; his father was cold and unfeeling. Kurt hugged Kory to him hard; he'd been worried about Kory being stuck with his parents. Kory had tried to leave right after he graduated from high school and had gotten dragged into being a camp counselor instead of starting college. Kurt's mother was just as bad as Austin's, if not worse. They'd had their mouths cleaned out with soap as children for saying 'damn' and been beaten with a stick if their chores hadn't gotten done. Kurt had never been so relieved to see his brother.

"How are you, Nugget?" Kurt walked with Kory to the door of their unit.

"I'm about to run away from home! Be glad you left when you did; Mom's worse than ever and I can't do another summer of 'gays are bad' camp," Kory said.

"Jesus," Austin's eyes went wide. "Really? I thought my family was bad."

"Please tell me you stopped buying all that shit, bro. If I have to listen to one more lecture on the sins of the flesh..." Kory rolled his eyes.

Austin cracked up. "Well, your brother and I go out to gay clubs all the time, with gay men."

Kory's eyes almost popped out of his head. Kurt had to laugh. "Breathe!"

"*Really?*" Kory looked at his brother in utter disbelief.

"Yes, really. In fact we are going out tomorrow night with friends. You are more than welcome to tag along," Kurt said, as he unlocked the door to their unit. "You guys drove out here?"

"Yep," Kory nodded. "Imagine how much fun *that* was."

"Why didn't you just fly out on your own?" Kurt asked.

Kory let out a gasp and covered his mouth in mock shock. "Are you serious? I could have one of those homosexual flight attendants put a date rape drug in my Coke and they could have their wicked way with me in the tiny bathroom!"

Austin bent over laughing. "Oh my God! Are you fucking serious?"

"Yep." Kory held his hand skyward. "God's honest truth."

Kurt shook his head. "Unbelievable."

Kory walked into the cool condo and looked around. Definitely a bachelor pad. NFL team pennants lined the wall and a large flat screen TV sat on one side. One long couch was positioned in front of it, with bean bags off to the side. A card table sat nearby with poker chips lined up in neat rows. Kory walked through every room, taking in the décor.

"Wow, you guys are so lucky." Kory walked into the kitchen when he was done.

"You can have the office, it has a futon," Kurt handed his brother a soda. "You okay with being on your own for a few hours? Austin and I just got off shift and need sleep."

"Yeah, it's cool. You have cable or sumthin'?" Kory asked.

"We've got satellite," Austin waggled his brows. "And an Xbox."

"I love you guys, I really do," Kory put his arms out. "Group hug."

Austin cracked up as Kory pulled him into a hug. "Okay, I'm off to bed; I'm dead standing on my feet. See you *much* later Kory," Austin waved walking down the hall.

"Night!" Kory looked in the fridge.

"You can have whatever you want; the pantry's stocked with chips and shit." Kurt mussed his brother's hair. "I'm glad you're here, Kory. I was really worried about you. I have to say I'm surprised; when I left home you were spouting hatred just like they were."

Kory's cheeks heated. "I met this guy at camp, a kid who was assigned to my cabin. I saw him when his parents dropped him off, they were speaking in a low voice to him and I saw him crying. Well, one night, after the kumbaya bonfire, I found him crying down by the lake. He looked scared to death when he saw me. He told me he was getting ready to kill himself right before I showed up," Kory shook his head sadly. "You want to know why? He came out to his parents, they told him he was going to hell and if he didn't come back from camp 'fixed' he wouldn't be welcome at home." Kory sat down at the kitchen counter with a loud sigh. "Who does that to their own flesh and blood? This kid wanted to *die*."

Kurt dragged his fingers through his hair. "Look, when I first got here, I still had the same mentality ingrained in me. Then I got to the firehouse and met Preston and Wyatt; I hung out with them at the gay club a few times. I was uncomfortable at first, you know? Then I realized that they were no different than most couples. Preston, man, he loves Wyatt with such fierceness," Kurt sighed, shaking his head with a smile. "We should all be so lucky to find love like that. It doesn't matter to me anymore that they are two men, because I see them as two human beings."

Kory sat back, mouth ajar. "Wow."

"What?"

"I just never thought I'd hear you say that. Too bad we're not Catholic - Mom could throw holy water on you and Dad would probably send you to the pope for an exorcism."

"How are you dealing with all this?" Kurt asked.

"I got the kid's number on the last day and when I got home I found him a support group in his area. He calls me once a month to let me know he's okay. His parents did throw him out and now he lives with his friend. Things have gotten better for him, now that he's free to be who he is. I think it just hit me like a bolt of lightning when he told me he wanted to die. No kid should ever have to suffer, or feel unloved, because of whom they are."

Kurt stood back, looking at his brother. "You've come a long way. I can see now why you didn't want to go back to camp with Dad. They practically instill that in the kids, that being gay is wrong."

"I think I want to start my own camp, just for kids who are gay and ostracized," Kory said.

"Well, maybe we can come up with something, okay?" Kurt hugged Kory. "I'm proud of you. I need to get some rest though; we'll talk more about this tonight."

"Yup, love you, bro."

"Love you, too," Kurt said.

~~

Tucker stumbled through the apartment door, barely awake. The night shift was having quite the effect on his sleeping habits. Wesley almost ran into him as they both headed for their bedrooms. Tucker hit his bed fully dressed, staring at the ceiling.

"When did you do this?" Tucker laughed.

"While you were at the store." Wesley came in the room and collapsed on the bed. "Cool, huh?"

"It's like you're flipping me off in 3D," Tucker tilted his head, looking at the huge middle finger on his ceiling.

"That's for leaving the cap of the sugar half on."

Tucker cracked up. "Okay, no more pranks for a while. I have to admit, you looked funny when all that sugar went in your coffee."

Wesley sighed heavily. "We need to make contact, Tucker. I can't do this anymore. Do you know how many nights I go to bed thinking about Kurt? How his eyes sparkle when I talk to him, his tight ass and those lips? I just want him, and I don't know how I'm going to make him love me."

"You can't *make* him love you," Tucker said. "Don't you think I want the same things? I

196

went out with Austin a few times, just as friends. It killed me to not hold his hand or kiss him. He's so damn beautiful. You and I both know we can't push this. The fates would not have given them to us if we didn't have a chance."

"We've been through so much already, Tucker. Your parents, my parents, running away and sleeping on the streets. We were lucky that Wayne found us; hell, we didn't even have to tell our parents we were werewolves and got the heave-ho for being gay."

"Have you ever… heard from them? I looked mine up a while ago. They moved to Germany when my dad got orders," Tucker said.

"No, and I don't care." Wesley closed his eyes. His parents had never been there for him and the night he'd come home, beaten and bleeding, had been the last straw for him. He and Tucker had been at a party with Preston and had gotten drunk. The next thing he knew, one of the men at the party was trying to have sex with Preston while he was passed out. He'd gotten into a fight and two more men had jumped in. Then the shift had happened and he'd screamed just from seeing three men change into wolves. They all had been bitten; Tucker had woken up and jumped in and then Preston had joined the fight. Between the claws and the teeth, Wesley was surprised any of them had survived. Then their first shift experience came. Wesley shivered thinking about it.

"You're thinking about it." Tucker turned his head, looking at Wesley.

"It was a long time ago, we were eleven."

"Yeah, I know. You're still thinking about it, though. We were lucky to have Wayne as a father, Wesley. He never judged us, taught us that being gay is nothing to be ashamed of. We are who we are today because of Wayne, and if he says our mates will eventually come to us, then I believe him."

"I can't move," Wesley sighed.

"Go to sleep, I'll make dinner later." Tucker closed his eyes, sleep came quickly.

~~

Kurt woke up to his alarm going off. He slapped it across the room and sat up in bed. Sunlight was streaming through the blinds; he really needed to invest in thick curtains. He threw his legs over the bed and stretched his muscles. The smell of coffee invaded his senses, making him move. Throwing on some pajama pants, Kurt made his way into the kitchen to find Kory making breakfast. He'd woken up at ten to find Kory and Austin playing video games; after that, he'd gone back to bed. The whole day had taken a toll on his body, from the fire to his father. Kurt grabbed a coffee cup and looked over his brother's shoulder.

"Smells good."

Kory smiled, looking over his shoulder. "I can cook, I cook better than Mom."

"Well that's no feat. She sucks," Kurt laughed, sitting down. "Austin still passed out?"

"Yeah, I kicked his ass up and down your living room," Kory chuckled. "He's good, he's just not me." Kory turned around, spatula in hand. "He's really nice; I saw Dad's face yesterday when you said he was your roommate."

Kurt rolled his eyes, sipping his coffee. "Yes, because if two men live together, they must be fucking."

Kory's eyes widened. "Such language!" Kory pointed the spatula at his brother. "I'll wash your mouth out with soap."

"Damn," Kurt said, laughing.

"I swear, the more she forbade something, the more I wanted to do it. No cussing, no drinking, no dates until you're sixteen, no sex until you're married... blah, blah, blah. How am I going to know if who I end up with is good in bed if I don't test drive the car?"

Kurt almost spit his coffee out. "Have you... you know, had sex?"

"I'm nineteen, what do you think?" Kory said.

Kurt shook his head. "I so don't want to know about this."

"Okay, *Dad,*" Kory grinned.

"Ouch!" Kurt looked at his brother. "Fine, tell me all about it."

"About what?" Austin strolled into the kitchen, looking at the made coffee and breakfast on the stove. "He should move in."

"Kory was about to tell me about his sexual experience." Kurt sat back, waiting.

"Yeah? I need a good sex story," Austin said.

Kory looked from Austin to his brother. "Okay, so maybe I haven't had sex, but I've been thinking about it," Kory sighed. "I haven't had time to jack off, much less have sex. Mom's got me doing all kinds of shit around the house, and Dad has me at the church doing stuff. Believe me the myth about church girls is not true, at least not in Dad's church. I think he's scared them so bad they'll never have sex."

Kurt looked at the time. "Well, we should take you shopping for clothes. You can't go to the club in Wyoming clothing. We have some friends who love shopping."

"Yes, they bought Kurt Dolce and Banana," Austin snickered.

"That's Dolce and Gabbana," Kory raised a brow.

"Ha!" Austin cracked up. "Even your brother knows!"

"Shut up," Kurt smiled, looking his brother over. "Yes, Cole and Chaz will love you. You filled out, little Nugget."

"Yeah?" Kory said. "I started working out my freshman year; I knew I wanted to be a fireman. I heard the eight hour lecture from Dad about how dangerous it was, and not to make the same mistake you did," Kory leaned against the counter. "I think that's why he's had me so busy, working at the church, then at the camp. He's trying to get me to see his lifestyle."

"Yeah, well Grandpa would have had a coronary if he was still alive, the way Dad talks about being a firefighter," Kurt shook his head.

Kory eyed his brother's chest. "Nice ink."

Kurt looked at his chest. He had gotten more tattoos since moving to Seattle. "Yep, I keep getting them as a 'fuck you' to Dad."

"I want something Irish on my ass," Kory chuckled.

Austin laughed. "Let's eat, so we can shop. Club tonight. I can't wait for you to meet the guys, Kory. You're going to love them."

"I hope so," Kory said.

~REFLASH~

See how it all began with Mateo and the rest of the Skull Blasters as you take a journey that starts with: A Marked Man, Alaska With Love, By the light of the Moon, Half Moon Rising, Best Laid Plans, For the Love of Caden, The General's Lover and Russian Prey.

https://www.facebook.com/authorsandrine.g.dion

https://www.facebook.com/pages/Official-Sandrine-Gasq-Dion/137320826386776?ref=hl

3326630R00111

Printed in Great Britain
by Amazon.co.uk, Ltd.,
Marston Gate.